Samuel French Acting Edition

I0591867

The Behavior of Broadus

by Burglars of Hamm:
Carolyn Almos, Matt Almos,
Jon Beauregard & Albert Dayan

Original Songs by
Matt Almos, Brendan Milburn
& Burglars of Hamm

SAMUELFRENCH.COM   SAMUELFRENCH.CO.UK

FOR PRODUCTION ENQUIRIES

UNITED STATES AND CANADA
Info@SamuelFrench.com
1-866-598-8449

UNITED KINGDOM AND EUROPE
Plays@SamuelFrench.co.uk
020-7255-4302

Each title is subject to availability from Samuel French, depending upon country of performance. Please be aware that *THE BEHAVIOR OF BROADUS* may not be licensed by Samuel French in your territory. Professional and amateur producers should contact the nearest Samuel French office or licensing partner to verify availability.

MUSIC USE NOTE

Licensees are solely responsible for obtaining formal written permission from copyright owners to use copyrighted music in the performance of this play and are strongly cautioned to do so. If no such permission is obtained by the licensee, then the licensee must use only original music that the licensee owns and controls. Licensees are solely responsible and liable for all music clearances and shall indemnify the copyright owners of the play(s) and their licensing agent, Samuel French, against any costs, expenses, losses and liabilities arising from the use of music by licensees. Please contact the appropriate music licensing authority in your territory for the rights to any incidental music.

IMPORTANT BILLING AND CREDIT REQUIREMENTS

If you have obtained performance rights to this title, please refer to your licensing agreement for important billing and credit requirements.

THE BEHAVIOR OF BROADUS premiered in co-production between Burglars of Hamm and Sacred Fools, in association with Center Theatre Group, in Los Angeles, California in September 2014, under the direction of Matt Almos and Ken Roht. The script was commissioned by Center Theatre Group, Los Angeles, California. The performance featured choreography by Ken Roht, musical direction by John Ballinger, projections by Jason H. Thompson, costumes by Ann Closs-Farley, lights by Brandon Baruch, sets by Tifanie McQueen, props by Lisa Anne Nicolai, and sound by Jaime Robledo. The Production Stage Manager was Rebecca Schoenberg. The cast was as follows:

JOHN BROADUS WATSON . . . . Hugo Armstrong

ROSALIE RAYNER / CHORUS . . . . Devin Sidell

EMMA / LOEB RAT / WET NURSE 1 /

BURNA / CHORUS . . . . Rebecca Metz

JACQUES LOEB/HEAD TRUSTEE /

RESOR / BILL / CHORUS . . . . William Salyers

PHIL THE RAT / CHORUS . . . . Andrew Joseph Perez

ALBERT / CHORUS . . . . .Amir Levi

WILLIAM MCDOUGALL / BERTRAM /

JAMES / PITCHMAN / CHORUS . . . . Tim Sheridan

DEAN STEVENS / BUDDY FRANKLIN /

CHORUS . . . . Jacob Sidney

WHITEY THE CHICKEN / WET NURSE 2 /

CHORUS . . . . Cj Merriman

MARY ICKES / CHORUS . . . . Erin Holt

CHARACTERS

CHORUS

JOHN BROADUS WATSON

EMMA WATSON

WHITEY THE CHICKEN

PHIL THE RAT

JACQUES LOEB

DEAN STEVENS

MARY ICKES

WILLIAM MCDOUGALL

ALBERT

BERTRAM

WET NURSES 1 & 2

ROSALIE RAYNER

HEAD TRUSTEE

STANLEY RESOR

JAMES WATSON

BILL WATSON

BUDDY FRANKLIN

BURNA BUNSON

VARIOUS ANIMALS & OTHERS

SETTING

Several locations over the course of the life of John Broadus Watson.
Among them: Rural South Carolina, Baltimore, New York,
and Connecticut

TIME

1878-1958

ACT I

(A **CHORUS** *assembles and begins to sing. They wear country clothing. A projection is shown, unrecognizable at first and slowly coming into view.)*

[PROJECTED IMAGE: A baby with a hammer held over his head]

[MUSIC NO. 01 "LIKE AN EMBER"]

CHORUS.

WHEN YOU ARE BORN YOU'RE ALIVE
YOU DO ALL YOU CAN TO SURVIVE
BUT IF YOU'RE LIKE MOST YOU WILL WASTE ENERGY
ON THINGS YOU CAN'T KNOW
AND ON THINGS YOU CAN'T SEE
IT HELPS TO HAVE LESSONS TO SHOW YOU THE WAY
AND EXPERTS TO TEACH THEM SO MAYBE SOME DAY
PROSPERITY WILL OVERFLOW
LOGIC AND ORDER WILL GROW
YOU'LL KNOW THAT YOU KNOW WHAT YOU KNOW

(The projection can now be seen clearly. It shows a baby with a hammer held above his head. The hammer rests in the hand of the otherwise unseen adult.)

(One **CHORUS MEMBER** *becomes* **EMMA WATSON**, *a plain woman in country clothing. She goes into labor. Another, the actor who plays* **PHIL THE RAT**, *steps forward to sing. He is not in his rat costume and is dressed in country clothing like the rest.)*

[PROJECTED TEXT: Rural South Carolina – Late 19th Century]

PHIL THE RAT.	MEN & WOMEN.
LIKE AN EMBER	OOH
IN THE DARKNESS	
MEEK AND SMALL	OOH
BUT SHEDDING LIGHT	
TINY BABY	OOH

(**EMMA** *screams, gives birth to* **JOHN BROADUS WATSON**, *played by a grown man. He wears a baby bonnet.*)

JOHN BROADUS WATSON	
HE WAS BORN	OOH
IN DARKEST NIGHT	

EMMA. Come on, boy. Get y'self in bed.

WATSON. Okay, Momma.

(*Shift to* **EMMA** *tucking* **WATSON** *into bed. He is older – his bonnet gone.*)

EMMA.

BEWARE THE DARK BECAUSE
SATAN WILL BE THERE
REPENT FROM SIN OR ELSE
SATAN WILL ENSNARE YOU
IN HIS NET
OF FIRE
AND STEEL
AND TEETH
AND VATS
OF BLOOD
GOODNIGHT
SLEEP TIGHT
MY SON

(**EMMA** *turns out the light.* **WATSON** *screams. She turns it back on.*)

WATSON. Momma, can we leave the light on?

CHORUS.

LIKE AN EMBER THAT GETS TOSSED AND

FRIGHTENED AND THEN LOST AND
STRUGGLES TO GO FIND ITS WAY

SO HIS MOMMA, SHE WOULD GUIDE HIM
COUNSEL AND REMIND HIM
EVIL MUST BE KEPT AT BAY

> *(WATSON and EMMA come together. He wears a conical birthday hat.)*

EMMA. Happy birthday, son!

WATSON. I can't believe I'm twelve.

EMMA. You're getting awful big. Now listen here.

> *(As she sings the following, we see WATSON's father, PICKENS, with two NATIVE AMERICAN WOMEN.)*

YOU'RE OLD ENOUGH NOW IT'S
TIME TO HEAR THE TRUTH
YOUR DAD'S A DRUNK – NO GOOD –
AND HERE IS THE PROOF
HE HAS GOT TWO
NOT ONE
YOUNG INJUN WIVES
THEY FORNICATE
ALL DAY
AND NIGHT!
NOW HERE'S
A GIFT
MY SON

WATSON. A Bible? Thanks Momma!

EMMA. You gon' be a preacher, boy.

WATSON. I am?

EMMA. And whatever you do, you stay away from your drunk old daddy!

> *(Instrumental break where we see WATSON get caught up with PICKENS.)*

CHORUS.
LIKE AN EMBER THAT RUNS WILD

> BEHAVING LIKE A CHILD
> A FLAME THAT YOU JUST CAN'T CONTROL
>
> BUT HIS MOMMA, SHE FELL SICK
> WITH CANCER, AND RIGHT QUICK
> THE DARKNESS IT DEVOURED HER WHOLE!

EMMA. John, where you been all night? I ain't feeling so good.

WATSON. Not now, Momma!

EMMA. Are you drunk agin?

WATSON. So what if I am?

EMMA. I warned you about yer daddy! I warned you to stay away from the dark!

WATSON. I ain't scared-a the dark! And I sure as hell ain't gon' be no preacher!

EMMA. *(She staggers dramatically.)* Oh!

WATSON. Momma?

> *(He kneels by her side.)*

EMMA.

> THE TIME HAS COME, MY SON
> DARKNESS IS AT HAND
> HOLD TIGHT TO CHRIST, MY SON
> NOW YOU ARE A MAN
> WHO MUST BE JUST
> AND TRUE
> AND GOOD
> AND PURE
> AND RIGHT
> NOT WRONG
> IN EV'RYTHING
> GOOD LUCK
> FAREWELL
> MY SON.

> *(**EMMA** dies and exits somewhat melodramatically into a bright light. She leaves her Bible behind. **WATSON**, completely lost, clutches the Bible. He opens it tentatively and begins to read.)*

PHIL THE RAT.	CHORUS.
ALL ALONE NOW	OOH
HE LOOKS FOR COMFORT	
FROM THE LORD	
IN DARKEST NIGHT	

LIKE AN EMBER	OOH
IN THE DARKNESS	
MEEK AND SMALL	OOH
BUT TAKING FLIGHT	

> *(The stage has grown dark. A dim light remains on* **WATSON**. *He holds the Bible aloft and begins to speak. His focus shifts as though he's talking to a large group, but it's too dark for us to see them. We should get the sense he is a preacher now.)*

WATSON. ...Now some may say you ain't got no business with the Lord. That yer all jist dumb animals. Well I say I'm way dumber'n any of you. I'm way more sinful than any a'you. And the Lord didn't give up on me. He gave me comfort in my darkest night. He *gave* me my darkest night so I'd *have* to reach out to Him. He's that smart. And I'm tellin' you, He'll outsmart you too. Make it easy on yourself and kneel before Him. Surrender to His everlasting grace while you still can. *(He wheels dramatically on one listener.)* I'm talkin' to you cow!

> *(Lights bump to a wider look to reveal he is talking to barnyard animals. During the following exchange,* **WATSON** *gets more and more worked up.)*

COW. Who, me?

WATSON. You goin' straight to hell!

COW. I am?

WATSON. And then you'll be sorry!

COW. But why am I going to hell? What'd I do?

WATSON. You just chew your goddang cud all day and that's all you do!

COW. I'm a cow – what do you want from me?

WATSON. GODDANGIT COW! YOU BETTER BECOME A GOOD AND PROPER CHRISTIAN OR YOU'LL BE SORRY!

COW. *(Shrugs.)* Okay. Fine. I'm a Christian.

WATSON. BUT YOU GOTTA MEAN IT! DAD-BLAST IT I'LL SEND YOU THERE MYSELF!!

> *(***WATSON*** *looks around and picks up an axe or shovel or something else and starts to go for the* ***COW.*** *A small, white chicken named* ***WHITEY*** *steps in.)*

WHITEY. Heeeyyyy!!

> *(***WATSON*** *stops and looks at her threateningly.)*

WATSON. What?!

WHITEY. Um… I would like to get baptized please.

WATSON. Really?

WHITEY. Yep. By golly you done convinced me.

WATSON. Yer not just tryin' to save that flea-bitten cow?!

> *(***WATSON*** *lifts the weapon again, menacing the* ***COW.****)*

WHITEY. Nope! Nope. I really, really wanna do it. It seems really good.

> *(***WATSON*** *puts down the weapon.)*

WATSON. *(Taking in the gravity of it.)* You're my first convert.

WHITEY. Hallelujah!

WATSON. *(Referring to the other* ***ANIMALS.****)* These dumb motherfuckers wouldn't know Jesus if he punched 'em in the face.

GOAT. Hey.

WHITEY. So whatta I gotta do to get baptized?

WATSON. Come here. Kneel before me. Open your heart.

> *(***WHITEY*** *goes to him with great trust.* ***WATSON*** *dips his hand in a nearby bucket of water and holds it over* ***WHITEY****'s head.)*

Do you rebuke Satan and all his works?

WHITEY. I reckon.

> (**WATSON** *drizzles a little of the water on* **WHITEY**.
> **WHITEY** *shivers.*)

That's it?

WATSON. That's it. *(Suddenly discouraged.)* Well, I got one chicken to show for months of preachin'.

WHITEY. *(Trying to intrigue the others.)* Boy I sure do feel different though!

GOAT. What's it like, Whitey?

WHITEY. Kinda tingly. You should do it!

GOAT. Aw I'm just a dumb old goat.

WHITEY. *(Checking with* **WATSON**.*)* But Jesus saves everyone, right?

WATSON. Sure. Unless they're goin' to hell – COW!

COW. Now hold on there – tell me more about this tinglin'.

WHITEY. Well, it's sort of a warm feeling. Like on a cold winter's night when John brings out one of his mama's blankets and lays it acrost your back. Or when he shares his old corncobs with us. Or when he scratches the feathers on my belly. Sorta like that.

GOAT. I want it!

COW. Praise Jesus!

HORSE. Sign me up, boss!

WATSON. Well step forward and enter the Kingdom of Heaven!

> *[MUSIC NO. 1.1 "I SURRENDER ALL – HARBINGER"]*

> *(They line up and* **WHITEY** *sings as* **WATSON** *baptizes all the* **ANIMALS**. *Each leaves after being baptized.)*

WHITEY.
> ALL TO JESUS I SURRENDER
> LORD I GIVE MYSELF TO THEE
> FILL ME WITH THY LOVE AND POWER

LET THY BLESSING FALL ON ME.

I reckon you could save this whole county!

WATSON. You know, you're right, Whitey. But I ain't settlin' for no small potatoes.

I'll head up north! Why, Chicago is just bursting with sin!

(*He notices* **WHITEY** *staring at the floor.*)

What's the matter, Whitey?

WHITEY. (*Sniffly.*) Nothin'. I'm gonna miss you.

WATSON. Aw, I'll miss you too pal.

WHITEY. My chicken heart's fit to break.

WATSON. Oh. Well…why don't you come with me?

[MUSIC NO. 02 "UP THE RIVER"]

You can be my assistant soul-saver!

WHITEY. Do you mean it? I would be honored, sir. Honored!

WATSON. The world's a'waitin'! Time to make tracks, Whitey! Chicago, here we come!

(**WATSON** *and* **WHITEY** *march off to Chicago.*)

CHORUS.

UP THE RIVER DID HE GO
UP THE RIVER DID HE RIDE
TO CONVERT A SINFUL CITY
AND SPREAD JESUS FAR AND WIDE
UP THE RIVER TO CHICAGO
TO THE MOUNTAINS MADE OF STEEL
TO A CITY FULL OF SINNERS
THAT THE POW'R OF CHRIST MIGHT HEAL

[PROJECTED TEXT: Chicago – 1896]

(*The* **CHORUS** *become Chicagoans.* **WATSON** *and* **WHITEY** *look upwards at the big city. They wander up behind a* **NEWSY**.)

NEWSY. Extra! Extra! Murder! Rape! Bloodshed! Only a penny!

WATSON. *(To* WHITEY.*)* We're just in time! *(He begins to yell.)* Salvation! Forgiveness! Eternal life! For free!

NEWSY. HEY! Get the fuck out of here.

> *(A* COMMUTER *approaches.* WATSON *steps in front of him.)*

WATSON. Hello sir! Would you like eternal life?

COMMUTER. No thanks.

> *(*COMMUTER *buys a paper.)*

Say, can I eat your chicken?

WATSON. No!

> *(*WATSON *grasps* WHITEY *and dashes away to safety.)*

CHORUS.
> BUT CHICAGO WAS A JUNGLE
> FILLED WITH BEDLAM AND DECEIT
> FILLED WITH CHAOS AND DISRUPTION
> AND IT FESTERED IN THE STREET
> BROADUS FOUGHT TO KEEP HIS HEAD UP
> DID HIS BEST TO SCRAPE ON BY

> *(*WATSON *comes upon a* MAN *pawing at a woman,* BESSIE.*)*

> BUT THIS NEW LIFE BRED CONFUSION.
> EVERY EFFORT WENT AWRY.

> *(*WATSON *chases the* MAN *off.)*

MAN. No no no no no no no no!

WATSON. He won't bother ya no more, ma'am.

BESSIE. *(Turning on* WATSON.*)* You shithead! That was my best customer!

WATSON. Your best customer should be Jesus!

BESSIE. Go to hell!

> *(*BESSIE *flips him off and exits.)*

WHITEY. Tomorrow'll be better…

WATSON. The only souls I ever saved was some barnyard animals who can't even get into heaven no-how!

WHITEY. Whattayamean? Ain't I goin' to heaven?

WATSON. *(Backpedaling.)* Now, see, Whitey, um…

WHITEY. *(Devastated.)* I shoulda known it was too good to be true.

WATSON. Whitey, come back!

> (**WHITEY** *runs* – **WATSON** *chases her through various brutal scenes of the city – drug deals, etc.*)

CHORUS.
> WITH A BIBLE IN HIS HAND
> BUT WITH GOD SO FAR AWAY
> IN A CITY FULL OF DARKNESS
> WITH HIS CHICKEN GONE ASTRAY
> BROADUS WANTED TO RETREAT
> TO PROTECT HIS TENDER SOUL
> FROM THE BRUTAL, SAVAGE PEOPLE
> WITH NO MEANS OF SELF CONTROL

> (**WHITEY**, *fleeing from* **WATSON**, *runs out into the street. Two* **THUGS** *appear, driving an automobile.*)

THUG #1. *(Seeing something else.)* Get out of the way!

> (**WHITEY** *is run over.*)

WATSON. Noooo!

> *(The* **THUGS** *exit the auto.)*

THUG #1. *(To* **THUG #2**.*)* What the hell was that?

THUG #2. *(Observing* **WHITEY**'s *limp body.)* It was a goddamn chicken!

WATSON. Hey, watch it! That chicken was my friend!

THUG #2. Well your stupid "friend" broke my headlamp! You owe me five bucks!

WATSON. I ain't givin' you nothin'.

THUG #1. Zat so?

> *(The* **THUGS** *proceed to beat the crap out of* **WATSON**. *As they beat him he says:)*

WATSON. No! No! Why?! Why you doin' this? Why?!

(As they exit they shout back:)

THUG #2. Yeah. Fuck you AND your dead chicken! Asshole.

> **(WATSON** *stands alone and weeps.* **WHITEY** *exits into a bright light as the lights transition and the* **CHORUS** *sings.)*

CHORUS.

> THAT OLD CENTURY WAS ENDING
> TIME WAS PASSING 'FORE HIS EYES
> AND THE SMOKE AND SOOT OF INDUSTRY
> WAS FILLING UP THE SKIES
> AND IT BLOCKED OUT ALL THE SUN
> AND IT DARKENED OUT THE DAY
> AND INSTEAD OF SEEING BLACK AND WHITE
> AND BLUE AND RED AND YELLOW
> EVERYTHING WAS GRAY

> **(WATSON** *stands on the edge of a bridge, getting ready to jump. An older man with a German accent,* **JACQUES LOEB,** *comes upon* **WATSON.)*

LOEB. Young man what are you doing?

WATSON. Leave me alone.

LOEB. Okay.

> *(Pause.)*

WATSON. I'm gonna jump.

> *(Pause.)*

Folks fight and steal and grope each other like it was nothin'. And just when you think it can't get no worse they up and kill yer best chicken.

[END MUSIC NO. 02]

There ain't none of 'em worth saving. And that includes me.

> *(Pause.)*

That's why I'm jumping. If you care.

> *(Pause.)*

WATSON. Ain't you gonna say nothin'?

LOEB. What would you have me say?

WATSON. Hell I don't know. Something.

LOEB. I thought you wanted me to leave you alone.

WATSON. I did.

LOEB. Okay.

WATSON. I mean, I did but geez…

LOEB. There are two possibilities at play. Either you will jump or you will not. Neither you nor I have any control over this outcome.

WATSON. What are you talking about? I'm in control.

LOEB. I would argue that you are on that ledge because of chemistry, biology and history, and that you are master of none of them. Free will is an illusion, my friend.

> *(Beat.)*

WATSON. Who *are* you?

LOEB. My name is Jacques Loeb and I am a professor of physiology at the University of Chicago.

WATSON. *(Snorts.)* The university! *(Mocking.)* Well how do you do! Bunch a peacocks struttin' round! It ain't nothing that's real.

LOEB. Young man, I am a scientist. I assure you that everything I stand for is very real indeed.

WATSON. Prove it then.

LOEB. It would be my pleasure. For this is the very nature of science.

[MUSIC NO. 2.5 "TO LOEB'S LAB"]

> *(Lights transition to* **LOEB** *'s lab.)*

Welcome to my lab. Where words become facts. Where ephemeral notions become concrete and real.

WATSON. Blah blah. Get on with it already.

LOEB. If you insist. Please allow me to introduce you to our subject. A distant cousin, if you will: the common rat.

*(A performer dressed as a white **RAT** enters the stage.)*

WATSON. I done seen a rat before. What's this gotta do with me and my free will?

LOEB. As mammals, we have much in common with this tiny rodent. Our nervous systems are organized in much the same manner. And much like us, these small animals possess emotions, desires, fears, ambitions…

WATSON. Rats have ambitions?

RAT. It's true. For example, my current ambition is to eat cheese.

WATSON. Huh.

LOEB. She perceives her will is to obtain and consume cheese, but this will can be manipulated, adapted, replaced.

WATSON. How?

LOEB. By controlling her brain.

*(**LOEB** takes out a saw and starts removing a portion of the **RAT**'s skull.)*

WATSON.	**RAT.**
Holy wow!	Hmm. Interesting. Interesting.

LOEB. I am simply removing a portion of its skull –

WATSON. Yow wow!

LOEB. To expose the cerebral cortex.

*(**LOEB** lifts up the piece of skull, revealing the **RAT**'s brain. Pause.)*

WATSON. Is that her brain?

LOEB. Yes.

WATSON. I ain't never seen one a them before.

LOEB. Secrets are hidden between the folds of this tissue. And now we will reveal those secrets to you, Mr. Watson. Where once this rat desired to eat cheese, now we will give her a desire to raise her arm.

> (**LOEB** *pricks a portion of the* **RAT**'s *brain and she raises an arm.*)

LOEB. And then lower it.

> (*He pricks again and the* **RAT** *drops her arm.*)

Now she will desire to stand.

> (*Pricks again and the* **RAT** *stands.*)

And take a seat.

> (*Pricks again and the* **RAT** *sits again.*)

WATSON. How are you doing that?

LOEB. By adjusting biology. Manipulating chemistry. Replacing history.

WATSON. Well, so what? I taught my hound dog to roll over and play dead when I was eight years old. This ain't nothin' new.

LOEB. Fair enough.

> (**LOEB** *pricks another portion of the* **RAT**'s *brain and she runs and grabs* **LOEB**'s *saw and holds it to her wrist.*)

WATSON. What are you doing?

RAT. Leave me alone!

WATSON. I don't wanna leave you alone! Answer my question!

RAT. I'm gonna end it all!

WATSON. Oh no! Why you gonna do that?

RAT. Because I'm tired of living that's why!

WATSON. Would you feel better if I got you some cheese?

RAT. I don't want your damn cheese! I want to kill myself!

WATSON. Dr. Loeb, we gotta do something!

LOEB. Very well.

> (**LOEB** *pricks another portion of the* **RAT**'s *brain. A change comes over her.*)

WATSON. You okay, Rat?

RAT. Am I okay? You bet I am.

WATSON. You want that cheese now?

RAT. Cheese? No. I want something more. Do you ever look at the world and think there's too much chaos? Too much pain?

WATSON. Yes.

RAT. Do you long to find a means of creating order? Of creating a path to global harmony?

WATSON. Well, sure.

RAT. That's what I want too. I think if I could make that happen, it would be better than eating cheese.

WATSON. Look at her. She's so happy.

LOEB. Her will has been altered.

WATSON. Well, whatever it is, it sure seems nice.

(LOEB *turns on* WATSON *with laser focus.*)

LOEB. Does it Mr. Watson? Even knowing that this renewed sense of purpose is only the result of a mechanical stimulation? That she is being operated just like a machine?

WATSON. Well, yeah, but –

LOEB. But WHAT Mr. Watson?

WATSON. If I have a brain that's similar to her brain…

LOEB. Yes?

(*Pause. When* WATSON *speaks, he has a calm confidence about him and his country accent is gone.*)

WATSON. Then I'm a machine too.

[MUSIC NO. 03 "GREAT GREAT MAN"]

(*Music begins to build.*)

LOEB. Very good.

WATSON. Fascinating.

LOEB. Mr. Watson.

WATSON. What is it?

LOEB. Your accent. It seems to have…changed.

WATSON. Yes. Yes it has. I'm a scientist now. I have a renewed sense of purpose and my path is clear. God is dead. And so I will now devote myself to the science of opening up the skulls of human beings so that I can control their brains and create harmony within them just as you have done with this rat.

LOEB. If only it were this simple. You see, Mr. Watson, this rat, as a result of having her cranium removed and her brain repeatedly punctured, has ceased to live.

*(The **RAT** dies. Music cuts out.)*

WATSON. Oh. I see. Well, that's too bad.

LOEB. Indeed, it is.

*(Pause. The **RAT** exits into a bright light. When **WATSON** speaks, the music begins again.)*

WATSON. But Dr. Loeb, remember when I told you of my childhood dog. How I trained him. The behavior modification was simple, attained through rewarding him when he succeeded and beating him mercilessly when he failed. Reward. And punishment. Perhaps there is a way to build upon this notion. To change behavior. Dr. Loeb, if I could figure out a way to control people's brains *without* killing them...

LOEB. Then you would really have something.

*(The **CHORUS** enters and sets up **WATSON**'s first lab at Johns Hopkins. They sing without irony. To him he is a "great, great man.")*

CHORUS.
    PEOPLE ARE LOST
    HE WILL GIVE DIRECTION
    PEOPLE ARE SAD
    HE WILL MAKE THEM HAPPY
    PEOPLE ARE WILD
    HE WILL TAME AND CALM THEM
    PEOPLE ARE MAD
    HE WILL MAKE THEM INCREDIBLY SANE

    HE'LL CONTROL THE WAY THAT THEY LOOK AT THINGS

HE'LL CONTROL THEIR MANNERS TO BE MORE NICE
HE'LL CONTROL REWARDS AND PUNISHMENTS
HE'LL CONTROL THEIR FEARS, EMOTIONS AND BRAINS

> *[PROJECTED TEXT: Johns Hopkins University
> – Eight Years Later]*

> (**DEAN STEVENS**, *the head of the Psychology
> Department, shows* **WATSON** *into his lab at Johns
> Hopkins.)*

STEVENS. This will be your lab, Watson.

WATSON. Thank you Dean Stevens.

STEVENS. As requested, we got you your two hundred rats.
(Mildly curious.) Tell me again what you hope to get out
of them??

WATSON. *(To him it's clear as a bell.)* I will be studying their
behavior and modifying it through a series of rewards
and punishments.

STEVENS. *(Doesn't follow.)* Oh. Good luck with that.

> (**STEVENS** *exits.* **WATSON** *shakes his head.)*

WATSON. Idiot.

PHIL THE RAT. Your work sounds intriguing.

WATSON. You think so?

PHIL THE RAT. Yes, absolutely!

> *(Beat.)*

You can understand me?

WATSON. Dr. John Watson. I very much look forward to
working with you, Mr...?

> *(He extends a hand for* **PHIL THE RAT** *to shake.)*

PHIL THE RAT. Call me Phil. Welcome to Johns Hopkins.

CHORUS.

PHIL WAS A RAT
HE WAS WHITE AND FURRY
PHIL WAS A RAT
WHO COULD LEARN AND LISTEN
JOHN WAS A MAN

WHO COULD MAKE CONNECTIONS
JOHN WAS A MAN
WHO COULD ONE DAY PERHAPS BECOME GREAT

HE'LL CONTROL THE WAY THAT PHIL LOOKS AT THINGS
HE'LL CONTROL THE MAZE AND LEVERS AND CHEESE
HE'LL CONTROL REWARDS AND PUNISHMENTS
HE'LL CONTROL HIS FEARS, EMOTIONS AND BRAIN

> *(The* **CHORUS** *becomes* **STUDENTS**. **WATSON** *is now in the classroom.)*

WATSON. ...and so, by administering an electric shock to the rat's genital area, it learns never to steal food again. We have altered its behavior through...*conditioning*.

> *(***WATSON** *accidentally bumps the desk of* **MARY ICKES**. *Her notes fall on the floor.)*

I'm sorry, Mary, let me help you with your notes.

> *(He picks up her papers and lingers on one. The* **STUDENTS** *sing its contents.)*

MARY.

HIS DEEP DEEP VOICE
HIS BLACK BLACK HAIR
IF ONLY HE KNEW HOW MUCH I CARE

FEMALE STUDENTS & MARY.

FOR HIS STRONG STRONG ARMS
HIS BROWN BROWN EYES
MY HEART IS MELTING WITH MY SIGHS

MARY.

I'VE NEVER SHARED
THIS MUCH BEFORE
I'M AFRAID OF POETRY

> *(Lights snap to normal.)*

WATSON. These are your notes.

MARY. *(Embarrassed.)* Yes.

WATSON. You seem to have a good grasp on the subject.

MARY. That's because you're an excellent teacher.

MALE STUDENTS.

> HER SOFT SOFT HAIR
> HER FAIR FAIR FACE
> PERFECTION FRAMED IN BRIDAL LACE

STUDENTS.

> WITH HER HIGH HIGH CLASS
> HER PROUD PROUD BROW
> A WIFE SUBLIME TO ACCEPT HIS VOW

WATSON. In the presence of those gathered here today, I acknowledge your new position as my pretty young wife. I pledge to provide all the benefits and services normally expected under these circumstances.

MARY. In exchange, I promise to provide entry into Baltimore society for my handsome and brilliant husband. And now that we are married, I will be dropping your class.

> *(Beat.)*

WATSON. Okay.

CHORUS.

> THIS GREAT GREAT MAN
> THIS GREAT GREAT MAN
> HE'S ON HIS WAY TO HIS MASTER PLAN
>
> THIS GREAT GREAT MAN
> THIS GREAT GREAT MAN
> A BRAND NEW AGE UNDER HIS COMMAND

CHORUS GROUP 1.

> HE'LL CONTROL THE WAY
>   THAT THEY LOOK AT
>   THINGS
> HE'LL CONTROL THEIR
>   MANNERS TO BE MORE
>   NICE
> HE'LL CONTROL REWARDS
>   AND PUNISHMENTS
> HE'LL CONTROL THEIR
>   FEARS EMOTIONS AND
>   BRAINS

CHORUS GROUP 2.

> THIS GREAT GREAT MAN
> THIS GREAT GREAT MAN
> HE'S ON HIS WAY TO HIS
>   MASTER PLAN
>
> THIS GREAT GREAT MAN
> THIS GREAT GREAT MAN
> A BRAND NEW AGE UNDER
>   HIS COMMAND

[END MUSIC NO. 03]

[MUSIC NO. 3.5 "GREAT GREAT MAN (PLAYOFF)"]

(The **CHORUS** *exits. Lights snap to reveal* **WILLIAM MCDOUGALL**, *a colleague and rival of* **WATSON**'s, *and* **DEAN STEVENS**. *They are involved in ESP experiments utilizing flash cards.* **MCDOUGALL** *holds a card that* **STEVENS** *stares at intently.)*

STEVENS. Ummm...hmmmm is it a...a...tree!

MCDOUGALL. Ah, very close indeed, Dean Stevens. It is a house.

STEVENS. Damn!

MCDOUGALL. *(Picking a new card.)* This time try not to concentrate so intensely. I find when the body and mind are relaxed it allows for a more elevated level of psychic penetration.

STEVENS. *(Attempting to relax.)* Right. Okay. It feels like an animal of some kind...is it...a...a...

*(***WATSON*** enters quickly, in a bother.)*

WATSON. Stevens! Someone has been in my lab again. I can't have it. The experiments require strict control... My rats –

STEVENS. Damn it, Watson, I almost had it. You could knock, you know. Maybe if you were a little more courteous with us, the rest of the faculty would be more courteous with your pets.

WATSON. Pets!

STEVENS. *(To* **MCDOUGALL**.*)* Is it a bird?

MCDOUGALL. Quite right, Dean Stevens. Well done!

STEVENS. Really? How many did I get?

MCDOUGALL. Two out of twenty.

STEVENS. Is that good?

MCDOUGALL. Yes, very impressive. *(To* **WATSON**.*)* I'm sorry, I'm being terribly rude. John Watson, I presume.

Professor William McDougall. Dean Stevens was kind enough to let me have a look at your lab. Such intricate and complicated mazes...the levers, the firetraps, the rotating blades! My god, I don't know what to call it.

WATSON. A maze.

MCDOUGALL. Right. Do your rats actually manage to traverse them?

WATSON. No. Not yet.

(Beat.)

MCDOUGALL. I see. Well, I myself prefer the maze of the human mind.

STEVENS. McDougall here has studied with Freud and Jung. (Excited.) Two out of twenty! That is good isn't it? I mean, it could have been anything at all on that card but I guessed a bird. What do you think of that Watson?

WATSON. It doesn't mean anything. Pure random chance.

STEVENS. Random my ass. It could have been anything...a ball, a bus, a dragon, a piano, eyeglasses, dice, keys, a tuba, a marionette, a pyramid, a windmill, bon bons...

WATSON. Yes, I get your point. Please continue with your game...and McDougall if you would like to visit my lab again, please make an appointment. I am sure you understand the need for a strictly controlled environment.

MCDOUGALL. Of course my good fellow. However, as it is, I don't think I'll have any more time for sightseeing. Stevens here just informed me that I've received the Hawthorne Grant.

STEVENS. I'm sorry, Watson. The trustees were truly impressed with McDougall's work on dream interpretation. It really is terrific. Go on, Watson. Give him a dream. You don't mind do you, McDougall?

MCDOUGALL. I'd be delighted. Allow me to set the mood.

(MCDOUGALL *reaches for a light switch and snaps it off.* WATSON *shrieks loudly and* MCDOUGALL *snaps the light back on.*)

STEVENS. Goodness Watson, did that noise come out of you?

MCDOUGALL. It seems our Dr. Watson doesn't care for the dark. I'd be happy to hypnotize that fear right out of you, Watson.

> *(**WATSON** calmly takes one of the cards, rips it in half in **MCDOUGALL**'s face, and exits.)*

STEVENS. Watson! You come back here!
*(To **MCDOUGALL**.)* He ruined your…guitar card.

MCDOUGALL. It was an antelope.

STEVENS. Dammit!

> *(Lights transition. **WATSON** returns to his lab and sets to work.)*

PHIL THE RAT. You okay? What happened out there?

WATSON. Nothing happened. Thank you for asking. Let's get to work.

PHIL THE RAT. Okay. I'll get it right this time, Doc, I promise.

WATSON. Trial 185. Begin.

> *(**PHIL THE RAT** enters an elaborate maze. **WATSON** is visible throughout.)*

> *[MUSIC NO. 04 "THE RAT I WAS MEANT TO BE"]*

PHIL THE RAT.
THREE STEPS TO THE LEFT
FIVE STEPS STRAIGHT AHEAD
FIND THE BRIGHT RED MECHANISM
SOON I WILL BE FED

TRACK THE SEQUENCE WITH PRECISION
STRIVE TO MAKE THE RIGHT DECISION
DODGE THE PAINFUL SEEK THE GOAL
AND MAYBE SOON YOU'LL FIND YOU WILL BE –

Ow! *(Beat.)* Hm. Well, that didn't work. What's wrong with me?

(A vision of **EMMA** *starts to appear.)*

WATSON. Trial 185. Failure. Come on, Phil. You're supposed to be getting better at this. What's the matter with you?

EMMA.

BROKE MY HEART
TELL ME WHY
CALLED ME NAMES
WATCHED ME DIE

WATSON. Snap out if it!

*(***EMMA*** disappears.)*

Look at the walls and the paths, Phil. It's right in front of you. Trial 186. Begin.

PHIL THE RAT.	CHORUS.
DO NOT LOOK INSIDE	HA HA HA HA
LOOK AT FACT INSTEAD	HA HA HA HA
DON'T LOOK TO THE HEAVENS, PHIL	HA HA HA HA
JUST LOOK STRAIGHT AHEAD	
TRACK THE SEQUENCE WITH PRECISION	OOH
STRIVE TO MAKE THE RIGHT DECISION	OOH
DODGE THE PAINFUL SEEK THE GOAL	OOH
AND MAYBE SOON YOU'LL FIND YOU WILL BE WHOLE	OOH

(Food rains down from above.)

PHIL THE RAT. Food. I did it. I did it!

WATSON. Trial 186. Success! Well done, Phil!

PHIL THE RAT. I don't believe it! I don't believe it!

PHIL THE RAT.	CHORUS.
I DIDN'T THINK I COULD	AH AH
BUT NOW I CLEARLY SEE	AH AH
THE FACT I HAVE THE POWER	AH

TO BE THE RAT THAT I WAS   TO BE THE RAT THAT I WAS
     MEANT TO BE!   MEANT TO BE

(PROJECTED TEXT: American Psychological Association – 1913)

(Music continues underneath the following as we shift to the American Psychological Convention in 1913. **WATSON** *speaks to the masses assembled.)*

WATSON. My esteemed colleagues, if I can train this rat, I can train you! You are both mammals – you can both be conditioned.

PHIL THE RAT & CHORUS.

TO BE THE RAT THAT I WAS MEANT TO BE!

WATSON. I challenge you here today. Give me a healthy infant and I will make him fear – anything I wish! A tomato... Or a microphone... Or this rat! And when I am finished I will make him love that rat again! Yes, through the application of what I call behaviorism, I have the power to control people's brains!

PHIL THE RAT & CHORUS.

TO BE THE RAT THAT I WAS MEANT TO BE!

[END MUSIC NO. 04]

[MUSIC NO. 4.5 "ALBERT (PLAY-ON)"]

(PROJECTED TEXT: Johns Hopkins University – 1919)

(Lights shift to **TWO WOMEN** *in* **WATSON**'s *faculty office at Johns Hopkins. Each holds a swaddled baby [the babies are both played by adult men].)*

WET NURSE #1. What does he want these babies for?

WET NURSE #2. Beats me. I'm just glad to get out of the ward for a few hours.

WET NURSE #1. Have you ever seen Dr. Watson? They say he's handsome.

WET NURSE #2. Yeah, but he's married. *(Small beat.)* Aw, who am I kidding – I wouldn't kick him out of bed!

(They laugh and then fall into shameful silence as **WATSON** *enters.)*

WATSON. Ladies.

WET NURSE #1 & #2. Good afternoon, Doctor.

WATSON. These are the infants from Harriet Lane Children's Home?

WET NURSE #1. Yes sir.

WATSON. Orphans?

WET NURSE #2. Or bastards.

WET NURSE #1. This is Albert. He's such a good boy.

WET NURSE #2. This is Bertram. He's good – when he feels like it.

BERTRAM. *(He takes her in.)* Hey, fuck you.

*(***WATSON*** moves to* **WET NURSE #2.***)*

WATSON. May I?

WET NURSE #2. Be my guest.

(He takes **BERTRAM,** *who immediately reacts.)*

BERTRAM. Um. Excuse me. Sir? Sir? NO! NO! NO!

WET NURSE #2. *(Shrugging.)* That's our Bertram.

BERTRAM. *(Screaming.)* DON'T FUCKING TOUCH ME!

WATSON. Take him back!

(She does.)

BERTRAM. *(To* **WATSON,** *in victory.)* Yeah, I thought so.

*(***ROSALIE RAYNER*** enters.)*

ROSALIE. Dr. Watson?

WATSON. Ma'am, I'm rather busy.

ROSALIE. No, I'm your new lab assistant, Rosalie Rayner.

WATSON. Fine. Take notation please.

*(***ROSALIE*** whips out a notebook as* **WATSON** *returns his attention to* **WET NURSE #1.***)*

Now, let's see what we have here.

WET NURSE #1. Albert is a dream. He won't give you any trouble.

(**ALBERT** *hums happily.* **WATSON** *picks him up –
holds him above his head.* **ALBERT** *stops humming
and calmly takes* **WATSON** *in.* **WATSON** *brings*
ALBERT *face-to-face and sticks out his tongue.
Nothing. Gives him a little shake. Nothing.*)

WATSON. *(Screams.)* OogaboogaOogaboogaOogabooga!

  (Beat.)

ALBERT. Everything okay?

WATSON. *(Talking to* **ROSALIE.**) He's good. This is a good
one.

WET NURSE #1. I told you. He never makes a peep.

WATSON. Yes – I think it will lend our experiment even
more credibility if we start with a very calm, secure in
– KA-POW!

  (He pretends to punch **ALBERT**, *but of course pulls
  his punch. No sound from the baby.*)

This is the one. *(To* **WET NURSES.**) You can take uh,
Bertram, back with you.

WET NURSE #2. Well that was a short break.

WET NURSE #1. Goodbye Little Albert. I'm sure Dr. Watson
will take very good care of you.

BERTRAM. *(To* **ALBERT.**) So long, sucker.

ALBERT. *(Open and innocent.)* Have a nice day!

  (They are gone.)

ROSALIE. Dr. Watson, I just want to say that I am so honored
to be in your lab and I will strive to be an asset. At
Vassar I earned a 4.0 average –

WATSON. I'd like to get started.

ROSALIE. Of course.

WATSON. *(Walks away from her.)* Prepare the infant.

  (Lights change as music begins. **WATSON** *steps
  into a pool of light.*)

At approximately nine months of age, the infant was
confronted with a variety of animals: a rat, a rabbit, a

dog, a monkey. The infant was monitored closely to determine whether a fear response would be registered.

[MUSIC NO. 05 "ALBERT, ALBERT, ALBERT"]

(Lights open on the stage to reveal **ALBERT** *and* **PHIL THE RAT** *facing each other at a distance. Perhaps photos and video from the actual experiment are projected through the following.)*

ALBERT.

SOMETHING'S IN MY SIGHT

AND I AM DRAWN TO IT

ROSALIE. *(Calling his attention to another animal.)* Albert!

ALBERT.

SMALL AND SOFT AND WHITE

I MUST REACH OUT TO IT

INNOCENT AND PURE

CAN IT BE SAFE TO BE

IN LOVE WITH SOMETHING WHICH

IS BUT A MYSTERY

(An array of **ANIMALS** *flood the stage and perform a dance of welcome as* **ALBERT** *slowly reaches out to* **PHIL THE RAT**.*)*

ANIMALS.

ALBERT ALBERT ALBERT

DON'T CENSOR WHAT YOU FEEL

WE'RE HERE TO BE YOUR BUDDIES

IN THE FACE OF YOUR ORDEAL

TOUCH US TOUCH US TOUCH US

AFFECTION WE REVEAL

THE FUR YOU TOUCH BETWEEN YOUR FINGERS

PROVES THAT LOVE IS REAL

*(***WATSON** *steps into his pool of light.)*

WATSON. After a week of testing, our observations remain consistent. Upon introduction of stimulus, subject's pupils dilate, with a marked flushing of the cheeks and a gentle cooing sound, all recognizable pleasure responses. There is no sign of any innate fear in this child.

> *(Lights return to the stage, where the* **ANIMALS** *dance around* **ALBERT** *and* **PHIL THE RAT**.*)*

ALBERT.

TOUCHING YOU IS GOOD

ANIMALS.

IT'S VERY GOOD!

ALBERT.

AND IT'S DEVOID OF PAIN

ANIMALS.

DEVOID OF PAIN

PHIL THE RAT.

TOUCH ME ALL YOU WANT

ANIMALS.

ALL YOU WANT!

PHIL THE RAT.

AND I WILL NOT COMPLAIN

ANIMALS.

NO, NO, NO, NO, NO

ALBERT & PHIL THE RAT.	**ANIMALS.**
FRIENDSHIP BE OUR SONG	OOH
AND WE SHALL SING IT THROUGH	OOH, OOH, OOH

ALBERT.

AND PRAISE THE LEAP I TOOK

ANIMALS.

PRAISE THE LEAP YOU TOOK

ALBERT.

WHEN I REACHED OUT TO YOU

ANIMALS.

OUT TO YOU!

> *(***ALBERT** *joins their ecstatic dance.*)*

ALBERT ALBERT ALBERT

REJOICE IN WHAT YOU FEEL

YOUR BUDDIES WILL STAND BY YOU

IN THE FACE OF YOUR ORDEAL
TOUCH US TOUCH US TOUCH US
OUR BOND IS STRONG AS STEEL
THE FUR YOU TOUCH BETWEEN YOUR FINGERS
PROVES THAT LOVE IS REAL

> *[END MUSIC NO. 05]*

> *[MUSIC NO. 5.5 "ALBERT (PLAYOFF)"]*

> *(The* **ANIMALS** *all exit, with the exception of* **PHIL THE RAT**. **WATSON** *enters with great authority.)*

WATSON. Good morning, little Albert.

ALBERT. Oh, good morning!

WATSON. Ready for another day?

ALBERT. You bet I am.

WATSON. Excellent. *(Calling to* **ROSALIE**.) Ms. Rayner?

ROSALIE. *(Entering.)* Here I am, Dr. Watson.

WATSON. Take note. We have observed the subject has no innate fear of this, or indeed any, animal. It is time. Today, we shall add the stimulus.

ROSALIE. *(Handing items to* **WATSON**.) Of course, Doctor. One steel bar, eighteen inches in length and one inch in diameter. And a hammer.

WATSON. Remove the rat.

> *(***ROSALIE*** leads* **PHIL THE RAT** *away from* **ALBERT**.)

PHIL THE RAT. Oh, here we go.

ALBERT. Get back over here, silly.

PHIL THE RAT. On my way, kiddo.

> *(***PHIL THE RAT*** heads back over to* **ALBERT**. *Just as* **ALBERT** *touches him,* **WATSON** *clangs a metal bar with a hammer behind him.)*

ALBERT. Whoa! What the heck is THAT?

PHIL THE RAT. It's…it's nothing buddy. You're gonna be okay.

ALBERT. Are you sure?

PHIL THE RAT. Absolutely.

ALBERT. Okay. Hold my hand.

PHIL THE RAT. Okay.

> (**PHIL THE RAT** *reaches out to* **ALBERT**. **WATSON** *again clangs the bar behind him.*)

ALBERT. Oh, my gosh!

PHIL THE RAT. Just…

ALBERT. That NOISE, don't you hear it?

PHIL THE RAT. *(Putting out a paw.)* Just hang in there, pal.

ALBERT. Okay. I'll hang in there.

> (**ALBERT** *reaches back and* **WATSON** *clangs again.*)

ALBERT. *(Shrieks in alarm.)* Aaaahhh! Cut it out, Phil!

PHIL THE RAT. *(Taken aback.)* Me? What are you talking about?

ALBERT. You heard me!

PHIL THE RAT. I didn't do anything.

ALBERT. Really??

PHIL THE RAT. NO!

ALBERT. Then why does it only happen when you come over?

PHIL THE RAT. I… I… *(Exchanges a look with* **WATSON**.*)* I don't know. *(He offers his hand.)* I'm right here.

> (**ALBERT** *reaches for him.* **WATSON** *clangs the bar three times.*)

ALBERT. GOD DAMN IT! GET AWAY FROM ME! GET AWAY FROM ME! WAH! WAH! WAH!

> (**ALBERT** *falls to the floor in a sobbing heap.*)

WATSON. Yes!

> (**WATSON** *is flushed with excitement. After a moment.*)

Enough. Remove the rat.

(ROSALIE *takes hold of* PHIL THE RAT *and leads him away.*)

PHIL THE RAT. Hey, gimme a second. (*To* ALBERT.) Honestly, Albert, listen… It's for science, buddy. It's for science!

(ROSALIE *pushes* PHIL THE RAT *from the room.* ALBERT *whimpers to himself.* WATSON *and* ROSALIE *are aware that something important has happened.*)

WATSON. Ms. Rayner.

(ROSALIE *does not respond, lost in thought.*)

Ms. Rayner?

ROSALIE. What? Oh! I'm so sorry, Doctor.

WATSON. Quite all right.

ROSALIE. Some observations?

WATSON. Yes, please. (*Examining* ALBERT *closely.*) Subject is now shaking violently, with histamine response now not only in the cheeks but about the chest and arms as well. The area surrounding the subject's eyes is inflamed and red. Furthermore, subject exhibits no small amount of drooling and running of his mucus…

ROSALIE. (*A sudden burst of confidence.*) John!

(WATSON *bolts upright.* ROSALIE *sees this and hesitates.*)

May I call you John?

(*A long, sexually-charged pause.*)

WATSON. You most certainly may not.

ROSALIE. Oh. Well, if I may say so – Doctor – you're handling of that situation was well…ruthless. Ruthless and masterful.

WATSON. Thank you. Now, where was I?

(ROSALIE *glances at her notebook.*)

ROSALIE. "Drooling and running of his mucus."

WATSON. *(He stares at her, ruthless and masterful.)* Of course. Now then, shall we continue?

ROSALIE. Ready when you are...Doctor.

> *[MUSIC NO. 06 "GREAT GREAT MAN (REPRISE)"]*

> *(WATSON turns on ROSALIE. They share an insolent stare-down as the CHORUS emerges, singing through the scene change.)*

> *(PROJECTED IMAGE: An in-house Johns Hopkins Faculty Bulletin)*

CHORUS.

> THIS GREAT, GREAT MAN
> HE'S BROKEN THROUGH
> A BABY CRYING AS IF ON CUE

> HE'S MILES AHEAD
> OF THOSE WHO DOUBT
> BUT THEY CONTINUE TO TUNE HIM OUT

> *(Music underscores the following speech as the setting transitions to a cafeteria at Johns Hopkins University.)*

WATSON. The ramifications of the work cannot be overstated! For the first time in human history, the control panel for the human brain has been revealed! Soon we will instruct the masses how to free themselves of all the unnecessary albatrosses that weigh them down – no more fear, loneliness, jealousy, nostalgia! There is nothing we can't accomplish. War. Injustice. Man's inhumanity to man. It is in our power to end them all!

> *[END MUSIC NO. 06]*

MARY. *(She wasn't listening.)* I'm sorry?

WATSON. I was – did you not catch *any* of that?

MARY. Something about poverty?

WATSON. You know, you really might do well to take more interest in this work.

MARY. Is that so?

WATSON. Yes. You have a few habits that could benefit from some rigorous conditioning.

MARY. Such as?

WATSON. Your compulsion to make expensive long-distance telephone calls to your maiden aunt in Pittsburgh.

MARY. Mm-hm?

WATSON. Your interest in the private lives of motion picture actors who are utter strangers to you.

MARY. Go on.

WATSON. Your love of that goddamn Victrola…

MARY. *(Exploding.)* Don't you start in on that Victrola!

WATSON. Those insipid records do nothing but spew forth a racket of romantic clichés.

MARY. I love it!

WATSON. And I could make you fear it just as easily.

MARY. Eat your breakfast.

WATSON. That's settled. I'm going to. I'm going to make you fear it. At six p.m.

   *(*MCDOUGALL *enters.)*

MARY. *(Ignores* WATSON, *demeanor changes immediately.)* Oh, good morning William! I hope you've recovered from your robust performance in the faculty cricket game.

WATSON. Cricket!

MCDOUGALL. You're too kind. What are a few sore muscles next to the prettiest cheering section in town?

MARY. Oh you do go on.

MCDOUGALL. Well, enjoy your breakfast. And may I recommend the danish today. It's yummy!

   *(*MCDOUGALL *moves away.)*

WATSON. "Try the danish – it's yummy!"

MARY. I don't know why you don't like him. I swear you're jealous because he was in the *Saturday Evening Post*.

WATSON. I was in *The Journal of Comparative Ocular Rodent Anatomy.*

(Gets an idea.) Check this out.

*(**WATSON** gets up and moves toward **MCDOUGALL**.)*

MARY. John, what are you –

WATSON. MCDOUGALL! I understand congratulations are in order. From you. To me. I proved that fear is a conditioned response.

MCDOUGALL. Oh yes. I saw your claims in the faculty bulletin.

WATSON. You're welcome to stop by and see for yourself. You do know where the SCIENCE building is, don't you McDougall?

MCDOUGALL. Actually, I do, Watson. My renowned hypnotherapy facility is there. Perhaps you've heard of it. I help people lead richer, happier lives. As opposed to spending my days frightening helpless children.

*(He reaches for his danish, at which point **WATSON** stabs his fork down into the table, almost but not quite stabbing him in the arm.)*

AUGGHH! What the hell are you doing?!

WATSON. Proving a point. Rest assured, the fork will never touch you.

MCDOUGALL. You're really off your rocker, Watson.

*(He reaches for the danish again, and once again **WATSON** nearly stabs him with the fork.)*

AUGH! I wish you would stop doing that.

(He has an impulse to grab the danish again, but resists it.)

WATSON. In a minute. What's the matter, McDougall? Does the pastry frighten you?

MCDOUGALL. No.

WATSON. Well then…bon appétit.

*(**WATSON** waits expectantly. Realizing he won't leave him alone, **MCDOUGALL** begins to reach*

for the danish, eyeing **WATSON**. *As he grasps it,* **WATSON** *stabs the table many times and* **MCDOUGALL** *flinches but keeps going and takes a bite of the danish as* **WATSON** *stabs the air around his head.* **MCDOUGALL** *grimly finishes the danish and then rises with great dignity.)*

MCDOUGALL. Well, congratulations, Watson. You've made breakfast perfectly unpleasant and proven – I don't know what – that you shouldn't be trusted around cutlery.

WATSON. *(Effortlessly.)* Look in your pocket. I've left you a gift.

*(***MCDOUGALL*** looks down at his pocket and sees a danish nestled in it. With the speed of an automatic response, he shrieks and begins to jump around, pulling the lab coat away from him to distance himself from the pocket's contents.)*

MCDOUGALL. Get if off me! Get it off me!

*(***MARY*** heads over to* **MCDOUGALL**, *pulls the danish out, and holds it up.* **MCDOUGALL** *runs from the room, screaming.)*

MARY. It's just a danish.

WATSON. He loved it – and now he fears it. *(Turns to* **MARY**.*)* See you at six p.m.

[MUSIC NO. 6.5 "GREAT GREAT MAN (REPRISE #2)"]

*(***MARY*** stands there, puzzled by her husband. They exit as the lights transition and the* **CHORUS** *sings.)*

CHORUS.
HE WILL TEACH HER TO HATE HER PHONOGRAPH
IF HE COULD DO THAT DANISH THING
HOW HARD COULD IT BE?
HE'LL CONTROL REWARDS AND PUNISHMENTS
THIS WILL SOON CHANGE EVERYTHING –

JUST WAIT AND SEE

> *(Lights transition to* **ROSALIE***, excited in the lab with* **ALBERT***. * **WATSON** *enters, holding the danish. As he greets her, he carefully places the danish in a baggy and labels it.)*

WATSON. It has been a most excellent morning, Ms. Rayner.

ROSALIE. Well, your day is about to get better, Professor Watson. Albert just cried at the sight of my sealskin coat with no accompanying sound.

> *(Beat.)*

WATSON. You're joking.

ROSALIE. I would never make light of behaviorism, Doctor.

> **(ROSALIE** *removes the coat she is wearing and hands it to* **WATSON***.)*

See for yourself.

> **(WATSON** *gravely dons the sealskin coat and heads to the pram.)*

WATSON. Hello, Little Albert.

ALBERT. How's it goin', Prof– *(Seeing the coat.)* Mother of Christ! WAH!

> **(WATSON** *is stunned.)*

WATSON. *(Removing the coat.)* Good god.

ROSALIE. What did I tell you?

WATSON. More, Ms. Rayner! Bring me that –

ROSALIE. Santa Claus mask?

WATSON. Yes!

> **(ROSALIE** *hands him the mask and he peers in on* **ALBERT***.)*

Ho ho ho! Merry Christmas, Albert!

ALBERT. Santa? Holy shit!!

> **(WATSON** *casts aside the Santa mask.)*

ROSALIE. Incredible!

WATSON. The fluffy bunny!

> (**ROSALIE** *hands him the fluffy bunny.*)

ALBERT. MOTHERFUCKING COCK SHIT!

WATSON. *(Throwing the bunny in the air.)* YESSSS! We've achieved complete transference! Each and every white fluffy thing ignites a deep, deep terror! Poodles, clouds, whipped cream! They'll all send him into a panic!

ROSALIE. And with no hammer!

WATSON. Oh, Ms. Rayner, we have done it! You and I, we will be remembered for an experiment that opened up a whole new realm of possibility for mankind!

ROSALIE. We?

WATSON. Of course. You will go down in history as the best laboratory assistant I ever had.

> (**ROSALIE** *grasps her abdomen and makes a deep, guttural sound, as if she's enjoying a really big fart.*)

ROSALIE. Ohhhh.

WATSON. What is it, Ms. Rayner?

ROSALIE. Oh Doctor. I believe I'm experiencing a certain degree of plasma seepage.

WATSON. Plasma seepage?

ROSALIE. Yes, there is definitely a marked increase in flow and viscosity.

WATSON. Plasma seepage...

ROSALIE. From my...well, you know.

WATSON. *(Puzzling it out.)* Plasma seepage... Plasma seepage...

ROSALIE. Oh for heaven's sake, Doctor! Must I spell it out?

WATSON. I'm sorry, Ms. Rayner. I'm simply not following you.

ROSALIE. PLASMA SEEPAGE FROM MY VAGINAL WALLS DUE TO VASCULAR ENGORGEMENT! There, I've said it. Are you happy now?

> *(Beat.)*

WATSON. Yes. As a matter of fact, I am. Very, very happy. In fact I am experiencing no small amount of vascular engorgement of my own.

ROSALIE. You...you are?

WATSON. Yes. I am. *(Beat.)* Too bad I'm married.

ROSALIE. Yes. Too bad. *(Beat.)* What should we do?

WATSON. We should proceed. We are scientists, Ms. Rayner. This is a laboratory. And a laboratory requires precision...decorum...and control.

> *(Pause.)*

ROSALIE. *(Another explosion of plasma seepage.)* Ohhhhhhh.

> *(Pause.)*

ALBERT. What the hell is going on?

> *(Suddenly, they pull apart and move to different corners of the lab. Lights and setting change to a more theatrical look.* **PHIL THE RAT**, **ALBERT**, *and the* **CHORUS** *assemble at center stage.)*

[MUSIC NO. 07 "PAPER AND PEN"]

PHIL THE RAT.	CHORUS.
WHY IS IT SO HARD TO SAY I LOVE YOU?	OOH, OOH, LOVE YOU?
WHY IS IT SO HARD TO TELL YOU WHAT YOU MEAN TO ME?	OOH, OOH, OOH, OOH, OOH, OOH
PERHAPS I'LL WRITE A LETTER THAT REVEALS	AH, AH
MY HEART TO THEE...	AH

[PROJECTED IMAGE: Watson/Rayner Love Letters – 1920]

> *(The music continues under* **WATSON** *as he recites a love letter.)*

WATSON. To Rosalie mine: Every cell I have is yours, individually and collectively. I can't be any more yours than if a surgical operation made us one... I want to kiss you all twenty-four of the hours and then I'd quarrel with the universe because the days are not longer. Let's go to the North Pole where the days and nights are six months each. Enclosed, you will find a graph comparing my feelings for you to those for my wife. As you can see, you are now nearly three standard deviations in the lead. Best regards, Professor Watson.

MEN.

MY HEART STOPS WHEN I TALK TO YOU
MY MOUTH WON'T WORK, SO THEN
I'LL CAPTURE ALL MY LOVE FOR YOU
WITH MY PAPER AND PEN

WOMEN.

DOO DOO DOO DOO DE DO DE DO

CHORUS.

EMOTIONAL COMPLEXITY
IS BEST ELUCIDATED WHEN
I CAPTURE ALL MY LOVE FOR YOU
WITH MY PAPER AND PEN

PHIL THE RAT.	**CHORUS.**
THE DAY I GIVE TO YOU MY LETTER	DOO DOO DOO DOO
I LIE DOWN IN MY LAB AND CRY	DOO DOO DOO DOO
AND EAGERLY AWAIT THE DAY	AH, AH, AH
WHEN I RECEIVE YOUR SWEET REPLY	AH RECEIVE YOUR SWEET REPLY

(The music continues. **ROSALIE** *reads a letter of her own.)*

ROSALIE. Oh John. Thank you for the graph. I'm so glad that you are mine. Hopefully this will make unnecessary the surgical operation you alluded to in your last letter. Your proposal to move to the North Pole is…intriguing. Are you suggesting that six-month nights will allow us to engage in prolonged sequences of sexual intercourse? If so, I will begin a rigorous program of calisthenics to prepare my vagina. Very truly yours, Rosalie Rayner.

CHORUS.

>OUR GRASP OF ENGLISH IS SUPERB
>DEMONSTRATED AGAIN AND AGAIN
>WHEN I DESCRIBE MY LOVE FOR YOU

MEN.

>WITH MY PAPER AND PEN

WOMEN.

>DOO DOO DOO DOO
>DE DO DE DO

CHORUS.

>MY HEART IS WILD AND MUSCULAR
>IT COULD BEST THE STRONGEST OF MEN
>BUT I WILL TAME IT JUST FOR YOU
>WITH MY PAPER AND PEN

PHIL THE RAT.	**CHORUS.**
NO ONE WILL EVER GUESS OUR SECRET	DOO DOO DOO
WITH EASE WE'LL LEAD A DOUBLE LIFE	DOO DOO DOO

CHORUS.

>WE'LL WINE AND DINE IN PUBLIC VIEW
>LINK ARMS AND KISS (AND CUDDLE TOO)
>AND YET NO ONE WILL HAVE A CLUE

WATSON.

>LEAST OF ALL, MY WIFE!

>>*[PROJECTED TEXT: Newspaper headlines: Educator's Wife Finds Love Notes, Watsons File For Divorce, etc.]*

>>*(Instrumental dance break. A few* **CHORUS** *members transform into citizens of Baltimore, passing newspapers, notes, dancing and laughing with glee at a mortified* **ROSALIE** *and* **WATSON***, who flee.)*

CHORUS.

>I WROTE TO YOU AND ONLY YOU
>WITH MY PAPER AND PEN

AND CAPTURED ALL MY LOVE FOR YOU
WITH MY PAPER AND PEN
WHY DID I GIVE MY LOVE TO YOU?
WITH MY PAPER AND PEN

[END MUSIC NO. 07]

[MUSIC NO. 7.5 "PAPER AND PEN (PLAYOFF)"]

(Lights transition back to WATSON*'s lab.* WATSON *is working with* ALBERT*, with great urgency.* PHIL THE RAT *hangs in the background.)*

WATSON. Albert, you need to focus. We have much to do today and little time to do it.

ALBERT. Okay.

WATSON. We are going to make you love your little buddy Phil again.

ALBERT. The rat? No, I hate that guy.

WATSON. But do you want this bottle?

ALBERT. Yes!

WATSON. Okay, then, here it is.

(Holds out the bottle but doesn't release it. Nods to PHIL THE RAT*.)*

Now.

*(*PHIL THE RAT *pops up, waves at* ALBERT*.)*

PHIL THE RAT. Hey Buddy!

ALBERT. Ahh!

WATSON. Albert, you can have this bottle if you let Phil touch you.

ALBERT. No way!

WATSON. Come on, now. You know you want the bottle. Keep going Phil.

PHIL THE RAT. Doc, he's not ready –

WATSON. I said go!

*(*PHIL THE RAT *starts walking toward* ALBERT*.)*

ALBERT. Ahhhh!

WATSON. That's right you're doing great, Albert.

PHIL THE RAT. Hey buddy!

WATSON. And… NOW!

> (**PHIL THE RAT** *begins to pat* **ALBERT** *on the head.* **ALBERT** *convulses in panic as* **WATSON** *wildly shakes the milk onto him.*)

ALBERT.   Ahhhhggggoobbbbboooodddddallllleaaaaf hhhhffffggggguuuuuhhh!

WATSON. Now take the bottle. Take the yummy milk, Albert. Take it, dammit! Milky! Milky!

> (**ROSALIE** *enters, carrying a letter.*)

ROSALIE. John.

WATSON. *(Still struggling with* **ALBERT**.*)* Not now, Rosalie! Can't you see I'm busy teaching the boy how to love!

ROSALIE. I found this in your box.

> *(Ominous music.* **WATSON** *stops what he is doing. He slowly and methodically moves to* **ROSALIE**, *takes the letter from her, and reads it.*)

WATSON. I'm being summoned. By the Trustees.

[MUSIC NO. 08 "TURPITUDINEM"]

> *(The space instantaneously transforms to the mysterious Chamber of the Trustees of Johns Hopkins University. It is exceedingly dark and shadowy.* **WATSON** *steps into a pool of light. Additional pools of light appear and into those pools step the* **TRUSTEES**. *They are mysterious figures wearing hooded ceremonial robes. They sing in ominous tones.*)

TRUSTEES.

OOH OOH OOH

HEAD TRUSTEE. So comes to order this emergency session of the Trustees of Johns Hopkins University.

TRUSTEES. What has been spoken is truth. What is truth has been spoken.

WATSON. I'm sorry but it's a bit dark in here. I wonder if –

HEAD TRUSTEE. *(Interrupting.)* Silence! John Broadus Watson step forward.

> *(*WATSON *does so.)*

Do you admit to your abominable transgressions of adultery and lust?

WATSON. I do.

TRUSTEES.

> HANG YOUR HEAD IN SHAME, WATSON!

HEAD TRUSTEE. Very well, then. It is the decision of this Board of Trustees that as a result of your reckless actions, you shall be… WRITTEN UP!

WATSON. Written up?

HEAD TRUSTEE. A copy of which shall be put in your personnel file!

TRUSTEES. Yea, for this is so.

WATSON. I don't know what to say. I thank you for your mercy and your restraint.

HEAD TRUSTEE. Along with this *negative performance review*, there are demands.

WATSON. Of course.

[PROJECTED IMAGE: Jesus Christ]

HEAD TRUSTEE. No longer shall ye live as a godless man. Each Sunday shall you attend Holy Mass and submit yourself to your master, the Lord Jesus Christ. Accept you this path?

WATSON. *(Deep breath – the notion of this sickens him.)* I accept.

TRUSTEES.

> GOOD ANSWER, WATSON!

[PROJECTED IMAGE: Rosalie]

HEAD TRUSTEE. In addition to this, you shall give leave to the young woman who hath led you astray.

WATSON. Leave Rosalie?

HEAD TRUSTEE. Accept you this path?

> (**WATSON** *bows his head, overwhelmed and devastated.*)

WATSON. I accept.

TRUSTEES.

> GREAT ANSWER, WATSON!

HEAD TRUSTEE. Lastly, from this day forth, cease you the study of vermin. Henceforth ye shall be devoted to the study of psychology in proper.

> *[PROJECTED IMAGE: Sigmund Freud]*

TRUSTEES.

> GLORY EXCELSIUS!

HEAD TRUSTEE. Surrender to the study of the human *mind*. The repression of memory. The envy of penis. Analyze ye our feelings – interpret ye our dreams!

TRUSTEES.

> WE WRITE THEM IN JOURNALS!

HEAD TRUSTEE. We are humans! We do not run through mazes nor seek we cheese. We are…complicated. And so ye shall abandon utterly this terrible affront to the unique status of humanity that is behaviorism. Accept you this path?

> (**WATSON** *is frozen.*)

Accept you this path, John Broadus Watson?

> (*Pause.*)

WATSON. I'd rather fuck my own mother!

TRUSTEES.

> GREAT CALAMITY! OHHHH! OHHHH!

> (*The* **TRUSTEES** *continue "Oh-ing" through the end of the scene.*)

HEAD TRUSTEE. How dare you besmirch the sacred counsel of this esteemed body!

WATSON. No, sir! How dare YOU interfere with the pursuit of truth, the sanctity of science. I pronounce this esteemed body to be full of SHIT!

HEAD TRUSTEE. Dr. Watson!

WATSON. And another thing! Your dreams are meaningless! And when you tell people about them, they are BORED!

HEAD TRUSTEE. Dr. Watson, you've gone too far!

WATSON. So be it. Consider this my resignation. Good day, sir!

> (WATSON *storms out. Music reaches its crescendo as* HEAD TRUSTEE *runs offstage, screaming with rage. Lights shift quickly back into the lab,* ROSALIE *waiting for* WATSON. *He enters, lightheaded, head in his hands.*)

ROSALIE. What happened, John? Are you all right? What did they say? Are we staying? Is everything going to be okay?

WATSON. *(Answering each question in quick succession.)* I quit. No. They were angry. No. No.

> *(Pause.* WATSON *looks up at* ROSALIE.)

ROSALIE. Oh my god.

WATSON. I think I'm going to vomit. My heart rate is increasing at a rapid pace – I'm perspiring suddenly – yes – I'm definitely going to regurgitate.

> *(He runs over to the trash can but doesn't vomit – just hangs there doubled over, panting.)*

ROSALIE. I've ruined you. I've ruined you. I'm going to kill myself!

> *(He grasps her dramatically.)*

WATSON. No! Now you listen to me! Hopkins is small-minded! We'll go to Harvard! Or Yale! Oxford! Wherever you want! They'll be clamoring for us to move our work there!

> (ROSALIE *smiles through her tears.*)

ROSALIE. Really?

(Beat. Suddenly, **WATSON** *falls to his knees.)*

WATSON. No. We're fucked!

(A long, silent beat. The crying is ended and now **WATSON** *and* **ROSALIE** *contemplate their future. Finally it's broken by:)*

ROSALIE. John, tell me what I can do.

(Pause.)

WATSON. There is nothing that can be done. I am ruined. And by extension, you are ruined. I am sorry, Rosalie. All that we have been working towards has been for naught. This world we live in. It is chaos and darkness. And it will continue to be so.

(Pause. **WATSON** *is on the floor. Rock bottom.* **ROSALIE** *stands apart from him and observes in silence until a musical note sounds.)*

[MUSIC NO. 09 "I KNOW THE STARS"]

ROSALIE.

I KNOW THAT WATER BOILS
WHEN IT'S TWO HUNDRED TWELVE DEGREES
I KNOW THAT PLANTS ARE FERTILIZED
BY POLLEN BROUGHT BY BEES
I KNOW A PIGGY ORGASM
IS THIRTY MINUTES LONG

PHIL THE RAT. Really?

ROSALIE.

I SAY TO YOU THESE FACTS ARE TRUE
YOU CAN NOT SAY I'M WRONG.

I KNOW
YOUR PATH
WILL BE STREWN
WITH FOOLS WHO WILL LAUGH
IN THEIR IGNORANCE
AND THEIR JEALOUSY

I KNOW

THAT YOU
CAN RESTART
YOUR DREAM ANEW

AS I KNOW THE STARS
SHINE LIGHT THROUGH THE HEAVENS
LONG BEFORE THE LIGHT REACHES HERE

STARS SHINE LIGHT AND
TRANSFORM THE DARKNESS
SO STAY BRIGHT AND PATIENT MY DEAR

      *(***ROSALIE*** pulls* **WATSON** *up from the floor.)*

It's not over, John. We can press on.

PHIL THE RAT. She's right, Doc!

I KNOW THAT I CAN RUN THAT MAZE
BECAUSE YOU TAUGHT ME HOW

ALBERT.

I KNOW THAT I'LL START CRYING
IF THAT RAT COMES NEAR ME NOW

PHIL THE RAT & ALBERT.

OUR FEARS AND LOVES WERE SHAPED BY YOU
YOU PULLED US FROM THE VOID
WE'RE GLAD TO GET THE FACTS FROM YOU
AND NOT FROM SIGMUND FREUD!

ROSALIE.

I KNOW

PHIL THE RAT & ALBERT.

WE KNOW

ROSALIE.

YOU THINK

PHIL THE RAT & ALBERT.

THAT YOU THINK

ROSALIE.

THAT YOU STAND
ALONE ON THE BRINK

ROSALIE, PHIL THE RAT & ALBERT.

UNEMPLOYED AND

FACING CATASTROPHE

ROSALIE.

> I'LL STAND
> WITH YOU
> AND TOGETHER
> WE'LL CARRY THROUGH

ROSALIE, PHIL THE RAT & ALBERT.

> AS WE KNOW THE STARS
> SHINE LIGHT THROUGH THE HEAVENS
> LONG BEFORE THE LIGHT REACHES HERE
>
> STARS SHINE LIGHT AND
> TRANSFORM THE DARKNESS

ROSALIE.

> SO STAY BRIGHT AND PATIENT MY DEAR

> *(The lab coat wearing* **CHORUS** *enters and backs up* **ROSALIE.** *)*

ROSALIE.	**ALBERT & PHIL THE RAT.**
I KNOW YOU ARE HERE	AH
TO CHANGE WHAT WE KNOW	OOH
I KNOW THAT THE WORLD IS	
WAITING	
AND WILL FOLLOW YOU	
WHERE YOU CHOOSE TO GO	
I KNOW THAT THE ROAD	OOH
WILL BE FRAUGHT WITH	
PAINS	
BUT I KNOW TOGETHER WE	OOH
WILL FACE	
THEM AS WE START	START
TO CONTROL THEIR	TO CONTROL THEIR
BRAINS	BRAINS

> *(A field of stars has revealed itself in the background. Through the following, in silhouette, we see* **WATSON** *kneel before* **ROSALIE** *as if proposing. He then rises to kiss her. The* **CHORUS** *gathers round.)*

ROSALIE & TWO WOMEN.	CHORUS.
STARS SHINE LIGHT AND	AH
TRANSFORM THE DARKNESS	AH OOH AH AH
LONG BEFORE THE LIGHT REACHES HERE	
SHINE YOUR LIGHT AND	AH
CAST OUT THE DARKNESS	OOH

ROSALIE.

WHAT WE KNOW SHALL SMITE	AH, WHAT WE KNOW SHALL SMITE
WHAT WE FEAR	WHAT WE FEAR

[END MUSIC NO. 09]

(**ROSALIE** *and* **WATSON** *exit triumphantly, the* **CHORUS** *following. Audience applauds as though the act has ended. During this applause, lights come back up on the far corners of the lab,* **ALBERT** *on one side,* **PHIL** *on the other. They are applauding too. After a while, they stop.*)

ALBERT. Wow. That was impressive.

PHIL THE RAT. Uh-huh.

ALBERT. I didn't know she had it in her.

PHIL THE RAT. Yeah.

(Pause.)

ALBERT. So what now?

PHIL THE RAT. I think the experiment is over. They're gone. And they're not coming back. You're going to go out in the world afraid of me. Anything that looks like me. Anything that feels like me.

ALBERT. Oh.

(Pause.)

Did that really happen?

PHIL THE RAT. Yes. That really happened.

(Pause.)

ALBERT. Oh.

> *(Pause. Bump to black.)*

End of Act I

[PROJECTED TEXT: Intermission]

ACT II

[MUSIC NO. 10 "YOU KNOW THAT YOU KNOW"]

(The slick Manhattan offices of J. Walter Thompson Advertising Agency. The **CHORUS** *enters with* **WATSON**, *in his lab coat. As they sing, the* **CHORUS** *members remove his lab coat and dress him in a suit jacket, symbolizing his move from the world of science to the world of business.)*

CHORUS.
YOU KNOW THAT YOU KNOW WHAT YOU KNOW
THE LESSON IS NOT TO LET GO
HOLD TIGHTLY TO FACT AND YOU'LL TURN OUT OKAY
JUST ASK GALILEO, HE'S WORSHIPPED TODAY
WE KNOW NOW HE KNEW WHAT HE KNEW
FIND THOSE WHO'LL LISTEN TO YOU
FORCIBLY TELL THEM WHAT'S TRUE!

[PROJECTED TEXT: J. Walter Thompson Ad Agency, New York City – 1921.]

*(***CHORUS*** exits. ***WATSON***, determined, enters the office of ***STANLEY RESOR***, President of the J. Walter Thompson advertising agency.)*

WATSON. Mr. Resor, I'm John Broadus Watson. I thank you for taking the time to meet with me. I promise it will be worth your while.

RESOR. I certainly hope so.

WATSON. I am not an artist. I am not a writer. I am not a number cruncher or a businessman. I am a scientist.

RESOR. I thought psychology was your game.

WATSON. As I was saying, a scientist. A master of cause and effect. What causes a child to grow up to be a lunatic? What causes a woman to go mad during her time of menses? These are the things that consume my interest.

RESOR. Fascinating.

WATSON. So I ask you, Mr. Resor. What causes a person to choose one product over another?

RESOR. Do tell.

WATSON. I'll tell you one thing for damned sure. It isn't this!

(**WATSON** *shows him an advertisement for Pond's Cold Cream.*)

RESOR. Say now, Watson, that's one of our advertisements.

WATSON. Is it now?

RESOR. A rather successful one at that.

WATSON. And what does it purport to inspire, pray tell?

RESOR. It tells the story of Pond's Cold Cream being a product favored by high-class dames.

WATSON. Let me tell you something about that story, Mr. Resor. It's BORING!

RESOR. What the –

WATSON. If I were a dame looking to buy cold cream, I'd rather get punched in the tits than listen to that boring story.

RESOR. I never!

WATSON. Now you listen and you listen good, Resor! We don't need to be told stories. Let's leave that twaddle to schoolmarms and nannies. We are men, you and I. Stern and proud are we. We inspire action. In short, we need to inspire these dames to open their pocketbooks.

RESOR. I'm not going to sit here and –

(**WATSON** *shoves him down.*)

WATSON. I'm not finished! There are three things that motivate action. Just three. Rage, love and fear. My advertisement taps into all three. What makes these dames feel rage? Getting passed over by a hunky beau for a prettier doll. What do they love? A hot sausage slamming up inside their love oven! But the most important question is what do they fear? Consider *this.*

(Lights shift to a stylized look on another part of the stage as music begins. A **PITCH MAN** *steps out and begins to sing. Perhaps a 1920s era ad for Pond's is projected somewhere on the stage.)*

[MUSIC NO. 11 "AD MAN"]

PITCH MAN.
LISTEN TO ME NOW O LOVELY LADIES
DO YOU WISH A BEAU WOULD TAKE YOU BY THE HAND?
PERHAPS THERE IS AN ANSWER, A WAY TO TURN THE TIDE
AND MAKE THAT BOY SUBMIT TO YOUR COMMAND

JUST TRY POND'S COLD CREAM
SOFTER THAN A SWEET DAYDREAM
IF YOU TRY IT YOU'LL LOOK KEEN
IF YOU DON'T YOU'LL LOOK OLD

OH DID I SCARE YOU?
I ONLY WANT TO PREPARE YOU
FOR ALL THE PAIN AND DESPAIR YOU
FIND WHEN DEATH WILL TAKE HOLD

[PROJECTED IMAGE: A testimonial ad, featuring a regal figure]

ASK LADY URSULA
WHY SHE'S ROYAL THROUGH AND THROUGH
A HUNDRED TIMES MORE ELEGANT THAN YOU
YOU WANT TO BE JUST LIKE HER?
BUY POND'S WITHOUT DELAY
'CAUSE IF YOU DON'T YOU'LL BE ALONE
UNTIL YOUR DYING DAY

(Music continues under the following.)

WATSON. Fear is a powerful tool. Be direct, Mr. Resor! Take advantage of this knowledge. Science is the engine that guides this behavior. And I am its master.

RESOR. Security!

> *(Slight pause – we think he's kicking* **WATSON** *out but then he calls:)*

Sales team! Steno pool! Art department! Mail room!

> *(The* **WORKERS** *rush in and assemble uncertainly.)*

Feast your eyes on this joker. He'd have you believe he's a scientist. But I don't see no lab coat, and he AIN'T NO SCIENTIST!

WATSON. OH YEAH? Well what am I then?!

RESOR. I'LL TELL YOU WHAT YOU ARE!!
YOU ARE AN AD MAN
MAKE THE SALE LIKE AN AD MAN
BLAZE THE TRAIL LIKE AN AD MAN
THAT'S THE TALE THAT WE TELL.

CHORUS. Go make the sale!

RESOR.	**CHORUS**.
IT'S OUR AMBITION	IT'S OUR AMBITION
TO MAKE A NEW PROPOSITION	PROPOSITION
WE WON'T PERSUADE WE'LL	
CONDITION	CONDITION
REWARDS AND PUNISHMENTS	
SELL	THEY SURELY DO!

CHORUS.
IT'S 1921
AND THERE'S PRODUCTS EVERYWHERE
SO MANY CHOICES MAKE IT TOUGH TO BEAR

RESOR.	**CHORUS**.
WE'LL MAKE THOSE CHOICES	OOH
CRYSTAL CLEAR	
AND TEACH THEM TO OBEY	OOH, OOH, OOH
AND AFTER THAT WE'LL MAKE A	
COUPLE	OOH, OOH, OOH, OOH
BUCKS ALONG THE WAY!	BUCKS ALONG THE WAY

(Instrumental dance break. **WATSON** *leaps on* **RESOR***'s desk and begins instructing the employees of J. Walter Thompson in rhythm to the music.)*

WATSON.

NOT THAT! NO NO NO!
TRY THIS!

RESOR.

INTERESTING!

WATSON.

THAT'S CRAP, MR. RESOR!

GIVE IT SOME FIRE!
GIVE IT SOME BLISS!

DON'T TREAD SO GODDAMN LIGHT.
YOU GOTTA ACCENTUATE THE FRIGHT.

KEEP IT TIGHT.
KEEP IT BRIGHT.

RESOR.

THIS CRAZY SCIENTIST HAS MADE ME SEE THE LIGHT!
GET OVER HERE, WATSON!
I LIKE THE CUT OF YOUR JIB, BOY!

(The **CHORUS** *of workers assembles in a row and pays homage to their new wunderkind.)*

RESOR.   **CHORUS.**

WE WELCOME YOU INSIDE   OOH
   J. WALTER THOMPSON

RESOR & CHORUS.

IT'S A REAL FUN PLACE TO WORK WE THINK YOU'LL FIND

RESOR.   **CHORUS.**

WE THANK YOU FOR   OOH
   REVEALING THAT
   SCIENCE IS THE KEY
UNLOCKING ALL THE
   SECRETS OF THE MIND   SECRETS OF THE MIND

*(***WATSON*** shakes hands with the staff – amid much back-clapping. A party atmosphere ensues.)*

ALL.

> NOW YOU'RE AN AD MAN
> MAKE THE SALE LIKE AN AD MAN
> BLAZE THE TRAIL LIKE AN AD MAN
> THAT'S THE TALE THAT WE TELL

AD MEN.

> GO MAKE THE SALE!

RESOR.	CHORUS.
IT'S OUR AMBITION	IT'S OUR AMBITION
TO MAKE A NEW	
PROPOSITION	PROPOSITION
WE WON'T PERSUADE WE'LL	
CONDITION	CONDITION
REWARDS AND	
PUNISHMENTS SELL	
	THEY SURELY DO!
'CAUSE YOU'RE AN AD MAN	HERE, THERE, PRODUCTS
	ARE EVERYWHERE
MAKE THE SALE LIKE	HERE, THERE, PRODUCTS
AN AD MAN	ARE EVERYWHERE
BLAZE THE TRAIL LIKE	SO MANY CHOICES MAKE IT
AN AD MAN	TOUGH TO BEAR
THAT'S THE TALE THAT WE TELL	
IT'S OUR AMBITION	HELP US, HELP US TO
	MAKE A CHOICE
TO MAKE A NEW	HELP US, HELP US TO
PROPOSITION	MAKE A CHOICE
YOU DON'T PERSUADE	OH, DOCTOR WATSON
YOU CONDITION	
REWARDS AND	LISTEN TO OUR PRAYER
PUNISHMENTS SELL	

> *(Suddenly, **ALBERT** is standing there. All action freezes onstage except for the two of them. The lights begin to fade, though **ALBERT** and **WATSON** remain in light.)*

ALBERT.

> STILL HERE. NOT GOING ANYWHERE.

STILL HERE. NOT GOING ANYWHERE.
THIS BROKEN TOY WAS
LEFT IN DISREPAIR

HOW DO, HOW DO YOU SLEEP AT NIGHT
HOW DO, HOW DO YOU SLEEP AT NIGHT
LIE BACK, SWEET DREAMS
DON'T TURN OUT THE LIGHT

> ***[END MUSIC NO. 11]***

> *(Blackout.)*

> ***[PROJECTED IMAGE: Times Square, New York City – 1923]***

> *(Lights transition. We hear crowds, horns honking, and urban chaos. A billboard begins to materialize behind* **WATSON** *that reads "Gobel's Meat Products – Healthy And Delicious – 4 Out Of 5 Physicians Agree."* **WATSON** *stands and observes the ad.* **ROSALIE** *joins him.)*

ROSALIE. It's wonderful, John.

WATSON. Thank you.

ROSALIE. It captures my attention and motivates me to action.

WATSON. The campaign is a tremendous success.

ROSALIE. Four out of five physicians. Such compelling data.

WATSON. I call it a "testimonial."

ROSALIE. Wonderful.

WATSON. I'm being promoted to Vice President.

ROSALIE. Vice President! I'm so proud of you, John. Johns Hopkins casts you aside and you could have crawled into a hole, but instead you emerge stronger than ever.

WATSON. I wonder.

ROSALIE. You wonder?

WATSON. Look out there, Rosalie. What do you see?

ROSALIE. I see...I see the lights of Broadway.

> *(Pause.)*

WATSON. *(Handing her a gift.)* I've got you a gift.

ROSALIE. What's the occasion?

WATSON. You are my love. And time is passing.

> *(Beat.)*

ROSALIE. Shall I open it?

WATSON. You know what I see when I turn my gaze upon these scurrying masses? I see an aimless crowd...aboard a rudderless, sinking ship...that is sailing across a sea of filth.

> *(Pause.)*

ROSALIE. Huh.

WATSON. I see ancient pyramids and temples on the verge of collapse. Look at them. The noise and the smell. Gasoline, sweat, food, excrement. The religion of narcissism. These people career aimlessly through life, flitting from one distraction to the next. Melodramas. Pop music. Sunsets and poems.

ROSALIE. Sunsets and poems. People are strange.

WATSON. They need saving. It is time.

ROSALIE. Time for what?

WATSON. Time to resume our work. *(A short beat.)* Open your gift.

> *(**ROSALIE** opens the gift to reveal a jar filled with liquid. A strange object floats in it.)*

ROSALIE. An embalmed embryo.

WATSON. Yes!

ROSALIE. Thank you.

> *(**WATSON** grasps **ROSALIE** by the shoulders.)*

WATSON. Oh, soulmate mine! This embryo signifies the child that you and I will have. The first child. The prototype. Do you understand what I am saying to you? Our home will become our laboratory. Together we will grow the perfect specimens of behaviorist children – rational, productive, happy. The neuroses our parents inflicted upon us will fall forever into the dustbin of history. And through our offspring, we shall teach the world.

ROSALIE. *(She smiles.)* Every cell I have is yours, individually and collectively. Impregnate me, John.

[PROJECTED TEXT: Three Years Later]

(Snappy, jazzy music plays as the lights shift quickly to a radio show in 1926, led by host **BUDDY FRANKLIN.** **BUDDY** *and his "dumb broad" assistant,* **BURNA BUNSON,** *sing the show's theme song.)*

[MUSIC NO. 11.3 "CAMEL SCIENCE SHOW THEME"]

BUDDY.

WHY'S THE SKY SO BLUE
WHEN I'M HOLDING HANDS WITH YOU?
DO THE CLOUDS RUN OUT
WHEN JOY RUNS IN MY HEART?

BURNA.

WHAT MAKES SUNSHINE FLEE
WHEN YOU'RE FAR AWAY FROM ME?
DOES THE DARK FEEL SAFE AT HOME
WHEN WE'RE APART?

BUDDY & BURNA.

OR PERHAPS THE ANSWERS LIE
IN ALL THE PHYSICS OF THE SKY.
THE CHEMISTRY, COSMOLOGY
THAT MAKES YOU WONDER WHY

SO LET'S SIT BACK ME AND YOU
AND WE'LL LEARN A THING OR TWO
'CAUSE THE CAMEL SCIENCE HOUR'S
ABOUT TO START

[END MUSIC NO. 11.3]

BUDDY. Once again, welcome to the Camel Science Show sponsored by Camel cigarettes. Our nation's top scientists have proven that Camel is the chosen cigarette of highly successful men. Do you want to join their ranks? Light up a Camel!

(Cheers from the audience.)

I am your host, science enthusiast, Buddy Franklin. As ever, I am joined tonight by my delectable assistant, Ms. Burna Bunson. Say hello, Burna.

BURNA. Hello Burna.

(Laughter. She lights a cigarette.)

BUDDY. This week, we welcome noted psychologist and budding child care expert, John Broadus Watson!

(Applause.)

WATSON. Good evening, everyone.

BUDDY. Hey, wait a darn minute! Looks like the doc has brought his two fine sons with him tonight.

WATSON. Yes, Buddy. I have brought them along because, I dare say, they are living proof that my scientific child rearing techniques *work*. William is two years old…

WILLIAM. *(Childlike.)* It is a pleasure to be here, Mr. Franklin.

WATSON. …and James is approximately five months.

(A small beat.)

JAMES. *(Like an adult.)* How do you do?

(Laughter and applause.)

BUDDY. Precocious little specimens, aren't they? Either these little guys have been smoking Camels, or the doc has cooked up some turbo fueled brain potion!

(Laughter.)

WATSON. Neither. With proper training, any child, even one as young as James, can be taught all manner of skills.

BUDDY. Care to show us what you mean?

WATSON. I ask you, Buddy, what's something every mother in America wishes for?

BUDDY. To never have to change a diaper again!

>   *(Laughter.)*

WATSON. Laugh if you wish, audience, yet behaviorism can indeed accomplish this seeming miracle. Both of my boys are long since potty trained.

>   *(Gasps from the audience.)*

BURNA. Get outta town! *(Small coughing jag.)* Even the baby??

BUDDY. I didn't believe it myself, Burna. So *tonight* – with the whole world listening – Dr. Watson has agreed to put his five-month-old baby to the test!

>   *(Music. A small, curtained platform on wheels is rolled onstage.)*

Doctor, if you would?

>   *(**WATSON** moves **JAMES** to the platform and situates him on the potty. When **JAMES** sits, his body is hidden but we can see his face.)*

Concealed discreetly behind this flowered curtain is a small children's potty. In one hot minute this little boy – who can barely manage to keep his head upright – will make or break his father's reputation on this tiny, harmless commode. Yours truly will narrate the action as it were.

James, are you ready?

JAMES. I am.

BUDDY. Then let's get to it!

BURNA. *(Holding up a stopwatch.)* On your marks...get sets... GO!

>   *(A starter bell rings.)*

>   *[MUSIC NO. 11.4 "SUSPENSEFUL POOPING MUSIC"]*

BUDDY. And we're off! Almost immediately, we see a look of gravity settle upon the boy's face, as if he *knows* the magnitude of what he is trying to accomplish! You know, ladies and gentlemen, for the half hour preceding tonight's show, James Watson was fed a special mixture of flax seed, corn and yogurt. There'll be no excuses tonight! Deftly, the boy's tiny hands grip the handles as his little body lifts ever so slightly. One can't help but wonder if he feels the pressure.

WILLIAM. *(Unable to contain himself.)* Focus, Jimmy! Focus!

BURNA. Twenty seconds!

BUDDY. Ladies and gentlemen, if only you could see the poor boy's face, the grimaces and contortions, the beads of sweat cascading from his brow, like a longshoreman lifting a heavy bag of grain in the noonday sun! Tension and release! Tension and release!

BURNA. Ooh geez, Buddy, I can't hardly stand it! *(Small coughing jag.)*

BUDDY. Quiet! It appears… YES! Everyone please, please give James a moment of silence!

> *(A silence falls over the room. We hear a few quiet, high-pitched grunts and then, almost sweetly, a single, clear note struck on a triangle. There is brief pause before the audience explodes into cheers.)*

Alright!

> *(Leaping to his feet, his arms raised in triumph, his head lolling about,* **JAMES** *heads to* **WATSON** *for a hug.)*

JAMES. I did it, Daddy! I made poo poo on the potty!

WATSON. *(Stopping him and instead shaking hands.)* Yes, you did, James. Very good work, indeed. A hearty congratulations from your father.

BUDDY. You hear that, ladies? No more stink under the nails. What do you think of that, Burna?

BURNA. It makes motherhood look so easy, even I can – *(Long coughing fit. She gives up, waves them off, and exits.)*

BUDDY. Yes. On behalf of women everywhere, God bless you Dr. Watson!

(Lights transition to **CHORUS OF HOUSEWIVES** *entering.)*

[MUSIC NO. 12 "MOM CHORUS"]

HOUSEWIVES.
REALLY LOVE MY CHILD
BUT HE WON'T OBEY
THEN A SMART MAN CAME ALONG
WITH A BRAND NEW WAY

RAISE OUR CHILDREN WITH PRECISION
HELP THEM MAKE THE RIGHT DECISIONS
HOW TO PRAISE THEM HOW TO SCOLD
IS HOW WE KEEP THEIR DESTINY CONTROLLED

(Lights up on **WATSON** *at a book signing in front of an audience of women.)*

FACILITATOR. Four out of five American mothers say John Watson's *Psychological Care of Infant and Child* has become their indispensable parenting Bible! Well, I think four out of five American women are crowded into this store right now! So please, ladies, if you have a question, ask it while your book is signed.

(The woman at the front of the line steps up. She is young and bright-eyed and clearly enjoys the attention of the room.)

[END MUSIC NO. 12]

HAPPY MOM. I just want to say that having children has been the greatest happiness of my life! I don't need diamonds or pearls – their little arms around my neck is all the ornament I require! Every time one of my little ones hugs me and says, "Mama, I love you –"

WATSON. Pardon me, but are you ever going to ask a question?

*(***HAPPY MOM*** didn't have a question, so she just stammers a little.)*

No matter, madam. What you are doing is wrong. Stop touching your children. This excessive hugging and kissing only weakens them. Look, I'm not insensitive to the fondness a parent has for a child – I have two sons of my own. A pat on the head is appropriate at times. Shake their hand in the morning if you like. In no time at all, you'll observe how independent and self-sufficient they've become. *(Hands her signed book to her.)* Thank you.

FRAZZLED MOM. *(Stepping up with her book, referring to* **HAPPY MOM.***)* I don't know what she's talking about. My kids are total brats. It's gotten so bad they just laugh at me when I spank them. I have no control. Should I hit harder?

WATSON. No. Certainly, time spent with children can drive anyone to violence. But *do not* hit your child. Physical domination, just like hugging, weakens the child. For this reason, rather than spanking, *(Looks up a passage in his book to show her.)* I advocate giving what I call a "Time Out." *(He hands her book to her.)* Good day.

REPORTER. Dr. Watson. Milt Whitmore from the *Baltimore Sun.* With all due respect, do you really feel you have any credibility to tell these women how to raise their children?

WATSON. Well, obviously I do.

(Titters from crowd. **REPORTER** *addresses them.)*

REPORTER. Do you know what became of Little Albert?

(Uncomfortable pause.)

WATSON. I can't say that I do. Ladies, I've just remembered I have another engagement. Please accept my regrets. I hope you'll keep in mind that by applying these principles, we are doing more than creating a happy child. We are creating a better future and a better world. I know you can do it. Thank you for your time.

(He exits to rapturous applause.)

FACILITATOR. Dr. John Broadus Watson, everybody!

[MUSIC NO. 13 "CONSUMER CHORUS"]

CHORUS.
>ONCE THERE WAS A VOID
>NOW THERE IS A BOOK
>A MILLION PARENTS WENT AND BOUGHT IT
>THEN THE PLANET SHOOK
>
>THEN THEY BOUGHT SOME SNACKS
>THEN THEY BOUGHT SOME SPRAY
>THEN THEY BOUGHT SOME BEAUTY PRODUCTS
>TO HELP THEM KEEP THE PAIN AND FEAR AWAY

>>(JAMES, WILLIAM, *and* ROSALIE *enter together
>>and take their place in a lovely park setting.*
>>ROSALIE *sits on a bench with a dazed and
>>concerned look on her face. The boys sing as they
>>toss a ball back and forth mechanically.*)

JAMES & WILLIAM.
>DO NOT LOOK INSIDE
>LOOK AT FACTS INSTEAD
>DON'T LOOK TO THE HEAVENS, BROTHER
>JUST LOOK STRAIGHT AHEAD

>>### [PROJECTED TEXT: 1935]

>>(WATSON *enters the scene and sits beside* ROSALIE.
>>*He gives her a kiss.*)

ROSALIE. How was your meeting?

WATSON. They want me to write another book.

ROSALIE. I just sent my article in to *Parents Magazine.*

WATSON. Oh, did you think of a title?

ROSALIE. "I Am the Mother of Behaviorist Sons."

WATSON. I like it.

>>(*He smiles and pats her hand. They sit quietly
>>together for a moment.*)

ROSALIE. I've been watching the boys all afternoon.

>### [END MUSIC NO. 13]

(Lights up on another part of the stage. The two boys are very mechanically throwing a red playground ball back and forth.)

WATSON. I see. They're playing catch.

ROSALIE. Yes.

WATSON. How long have they been playing?

ROSALIE. *(Looks at her watch.)* They've been playing for four hours.

WATSON. Did you say four hours?

ROSALIE. I did.

(Beat.)

WATSON. When you say they have been playing for four hours, I assume you mean a variety of –

(WATSON *watches the boys toss the ball back and forth.)*

ROSALIE. They have been tossing that ball for four hours. They have kept the same distance between them. As well as the same underhand manner of throwing. They have maintained a consistent three-second interval between throws. They have borne the same pleasant blank expression on their faces the entire time. They have not spoken a word. They seem utterly transfixed by this game. If one can call it a game.

WATSON. I think one can. The object of the game is to keep the ball from hitting the ground.

ROSALIE. Well in that case they are both winning.

(Pause. The boys continue to toss the ball back and forth.)

WATSON. They are good boys.

ROSALIE. They are, John. But I must admit this form of play…gives me pause. It is alien from what I remember doing as a child –

WATSON. Really? What could be more normal than a spirited game of "catch"? In fact, I'm going to join in on the fun myself!

(WATSON approaches the boys. ROSALIE watches.)

See now, my sons. I'm joining you. I'm joining your game. I invite you to toss the ball my way when you –

(One of the boys tosses the ball to WATSON.)

Ha ha! Splendid! Look out now!

(He tosses the ball to his son. His son catches the ball and tosses it to his brother. His brother tosses it to WATSON.)

I caught the ball! Do you see?

(He tosses the ball to his son. His son catches the ball and tosses it to his brother. His brother tosses it to WATSON.)

Again, I caught it. I excel at this game! And now for an enjoyable challenge!

(WATSON changes the direction in which he tosses the ball – tossing to JAMES if he was tossing to WILLIAM before, or vice versa. His sons freeze in place. The ball bounces off the son it was thrown to, as he makes no attempt to catch it. The two boys and their father stare silently at it. After a pause, WATSON picks it up.)

There is a lesson in this, my sons. We may toss the ball for an inordinate period of time. But eventually it will drop. It's the nature of the game.

Let's go, Rosalie. *(She doesn't answer.)* Rosalie?

(WATSON and the boys rush to her. As they reach her, they freeze in place. ROSALIE rises.)

[PROJECTED IMAGE: The article from Parenting Magazine, "I Am The Mother Of Behaviorist Sons," by Rosalie Rayner]

[MUSIC NO. 14 "I AM A MOM OF BEHAVIORIST SONS"]

ROSALIE.
   IN MY LIFE I'VE STOOD AS AN ADVOCATE

FOR WHAT'S RIGHT AND FOR WHAT IS TRUE
I'VE RAISED BOYS THROUGH SCIENCE AND INTELLECT
FOR THIS IS THE PATH THAT I KNEW

I AM A MOM
OF BEHAVIORIST SONS
SMART AND PRODUCTIVE
AND SECOND TO NONE

WILLIAM AND JAMES
MY BEHAVIORIST SONS
I CAN'T BE PROUDER OF ALL THAT THEY'VE DONE
BUT STILL I HOPE THEY MAKE TIME TO HAVE FUN

SUNSETS AND POEMS
WON'T HURT ANYONE

SUNSETS AND POEMS
WON'T HURT ANYONE

SUNSETS AND POEMS
WON'T HURT ANYONE

(**ROSALIE** *exits into a bright light.*)

JAMES.

NOW IT'S TIME
TO LEAVE FOR OUR BOARDING SCHOOL

WILLIAM.

I CAN'T WAIT TO SEE MY NEW BED

WILLIAM & JAMES.

LET US KEEP
OUR THOUGHTS ON ARITHMETIC
NOT THE FACT
THAT MOTHER IS DEAD

WE WILL EXCEL
IN OUR CLUBS AND OUR SPORTS
WE LOVE BOXING AND ROWING
WE NEVER COMPLAIN

JAMES.

SOME HOLIDAYS WE'LL SHARE

WILLIAM.

IF DAD HAS TIME TO SPARE

WILLIAM & JAMES.
FROM TRYING TO RESCUE
A WORLD FULL OF DARKNESS AND PAIN

> *(Music continues as* **WATSON** *takes a drink and wanders off, leaving* **WILLIAM** *and* **JAMES** *behind. The boys exit as lights transition to* **WATSON** *at a table.)*

> *[END MUSIC NO. 14]*

> *(He is on the phone. Across the stage another phone starts to ring.* **PHIL THE RAT** *enters the stage and picks up the phone.)*

PHIL THE RAT. Hello?

WATSON. May I speak to Phil the Rat please?

PHIL THE RAT. Speaking.

WATSON. Phil, this is John Broadus Watson. It's nice to hear your voice after all these years.

PHIL THE RAT. Dr. Watson? How are you?!

WATSON. Fine, fine. I wanted to let you know I'm debating that bastard William McDougall this weekend.

PHIL THE RAT. I hate that guy!

WATSON. Also, Rosalie died.

PHIL THE RAT. Oh my god, I'm so sorry.

WATSON. *(Beat.)* Yes. *(Shakes it off.)* Actually, if you're free, I could use a new partner. Someone to help me push forward my work. It'd entail taking notes. Maybe submitting to a few shocks to the old genitals here and there. Nothing too drastic.

PHIL THE RAT. A partner?

WATSON. Yes, Phil, yes! Twenty years ago we set off on an important mission. But we never finished what we started.

PHIL THE RAT. Yes, yes! I think about it every day!

WATSON. We planted the seeds but inexplicably they never came to fruition.

PHIL THE RAT. Absolutely.

WATSON. People's lives continue to be unpredictable, and filled with pain. The world needs us more than ever.

PHIL THE RAT. The world?

WATSON. Well. Yes.

> *(Beat.)*

PHIL THE RAT. Doc, I'm more worried about Albert. I mean, Christmas must be tough. Winter in general. Clouds. Whipped cream. Cotton balls…

WATSON. Yes, I get your point. But you're dwelling on *one* child that we programmed to fear very specific objects. Meanwhile, *millions* of children are growing up in generalized chaos and ignorance! *They're* the ones who need us. Surely Albert, as an intelligent young man, has realized that q-tips mean him no harm! And if he hasn't –

PHIL THE RAT. But *I* am the q-tip! Not you! I was his friend and I betrayed him. *(Calms.)* I'm just saying…we need to think about Albert.

WATSON. Are you coming to my debate? I can get you comps.

> (**PHIL THE RAT** *sighs.*)

PHIL THE RAT. Where is it?

> *(The stage transforms into the debate. Two lecterns are brought on.* **WATSON** *and* **MCDOUGALL** *enter and stand at either one.)*

> *[MUSIC NO. 15 "NEW YORK DEBATE SOCIETY"]*

> *[PROJECTED IMAGE: The logo for the New York Debate Society, plus a banner which reads: The Battle Of Behaviorism: An Exposition And An Exposure]*

DEBATE SOCIETY.

> WE ARE NEW YORK'S
> DEBATE SOCIETY
> WE FIND TWO SMART PEOPLE
>
> WE ARE NEW YORK'S

DEBATE SOCIETY
THEN WE WATCH THEM FIGHT

> *(Lights shift to* **WATSON** *concluding his opening remarks.)*

WATSON. ...In closing, to accept this theory fully and freely requires the courage to cast aside old habits. Behaviorism is new wine that cannot be poured into old bottles. Thank you.

> *(Applause from the* **DEBATE SOCIETY**.*)*

MCDOUGALL. Let me start by saying that I feel sorry for my former colleague. John Broadus Watson is a good man who simply hasn't yet summoned up the moral courage to admit he made mistakes.

WATSON. *(Mocking.)* Moral courage? Such *cruelty*, Professor.

MCDOUGALL. Ladies and gentlemen, allow me to draw your attention to Dr. Watson's most renowned scientific experiment.

WATSON. William, I hope you're not –

MCDOUGALL. His 1920 study on Conditioned Emotional Responses involved the veritable torture of a helpless little child –

WATSON. William –

MCDOUGALL. – the purpose of which was to make the poor boy fear things he had no reason to fear.

WATSON. You know *damn well* our intention was to remove that fear.

MCDOUGALL. But you didn't, did you? Ladies and gentlemen, is there *any* reason that will suffice? If any of you came across a child in emotional distress, would you not relieve it? But where you and I see a wounded child, he sees a machine with no inner life. Is that not true?

WATSON. Behaviorism is new wine that cannot be poured into old bottles.

MCDOUGALL. You said that already. *(Audience laughs.)* Let me say one last thing. There is a word for people like you, Dr. Watson, people who never had the impact they desired. That word, my friends, is obsolete.

(**WATSON** *suddenly and dramatically pulls the twenty-year-old bagged danish from his jacket and holds it over his head.*)

WATSON. Behold!

[*MUSIC NO. 15.1 "THE DANISH & THE QUEST"*]

(**MCDOUGALL** *falls to his knees in terror.*)

MCDOUGALL. Aaaagggghhhh!!

WATSON. Yes, McDougall, yes! It is the danish which I taught you to fear those many years ago. How callously you spit in the face of science when its power is utterly absolute.

(**WATSON** *stuffs the danish in* **MCDOUGALL***'s mouth. The* **CHORUS** *hums quietly under the following dialogue.*)

(*To the* **DEBATE SOCIETY**.) I have made my case over and over again. If you require irrefutable proof, then you leave me no choice but to supply it. Good day.

(*We see* **PHIL THE RAT** *moving through the audience, attempting to make his way toward* **WATSON**. **MCDOUGALL** *and the others file out.* **PHIL THE RAT** *gets to* **WATSON**.)

PHIL THE RAT. Dr. Watson!

WATSON. Oh FUCK, you saw that?

PHIL THE RAT. You were great!

WATSON. You were right, Phil. We have to find that kid!

PHIL THE RAT. Good, because I've assembled a crack team. You remember Shaky, Limpy and Toothless Joe.

(**RATS** *emerge from around the theater. All are tagged and maimed in some way – missing an ear, walking with crutches, shaking, toothless, etc. The final one is scratching himself fruitlessly.*)

ITCHY. Don't forget about Itchy!

PHIL THE RAT. The trip will take many years. It will involve crossing mountains, fording streams. Many of us will die – but still, we will follow you.

LIMPY. We shall find the child.

SHAKY. The child who has been lost.

TOOTHLESS JOE. We shall redeem him. And through his redemption, we shall be delivered. Pledge we one and all –

RATS. We will serve you, Dr. Watson!

WATSON. And I...shall lead you. Let's go! *(The music abruptly stops.)* But wait! I've got children of my own! A quick stop at the Holton Arms Prep School and we're off.

> *(***WATSON*** *and the* ***RATS*** *circle around and come to his* ***BOYS***, *who are playing catch in their usual manner. When he calls to them, they stop playing and turn their heads toward him.)*

Boys! Your father is going on a trip. I may be gone a long time. Ah... There's no time. Just...study hard. Avoid masturbation – it's selfish to your sexual partners. And stay out of the theatre. Okay then. You are men now. Goodbye.

> *(They resume their game.* ***WATSON*** *and the team embark on their quest.)*

> *[MUSIC NO. 16 "UP THE RIVER (REPRISE)"]*

RATS.

> UP THE RIVER WE WILL SAIL
> UP THE MOUNTAIN WE WILL CLIMB
> FROM THE GOLDEN LIGHT OF MORNING
> 'TIL THE DARK OF EVENING TIME

> UP THE OCEAN WE WILL SAIL
> UP THE ROADWAY WE WILL DRIVE
> WE WILL FIND THE CHILD WHO LOST US
> AND OUR HOPE WILL STAY ALIVE

ITCHY.

> I THOUGHT MAYBE I'D SPY HIM
> IF I LOOKED DOWN FROM THE SKY
> SO I HITCHED A RIDE ABOARD THE HINDENBURG

MALE CHORUS MEMBER #1. Boom!

> *[PROJECTED IMAGE: Hindenburg]*

> *(The* **CHORUS** *screams.)*

MALE CHORUS #2. Oh, the humanity!

TOOTHLESS JOE.

> I THOUGHT I SAW HIS FOOTPRINTS IN THE
> SAND BY THE SEA
> I THINK THE BEACH'S NAME WAS NORMANDY

> *[PROJECTED IMAGE: D-Day]*

> *(Man-made sound effect: gunfire!)*

LIMPY & SHAKY.

> WE LOOKED AROUND IN GERMANY
> BUT DIDN'T GET TOO FAR
> 'CAUSE AN IRON CURTAIN LANDED ON OUR HEAD

> *[PROJECTED IMAGE: Berlin Wall]*

MALE CHORUS #1.

> CLANG!

LIMPY & SHAKY.

> OW!

LIMPY, SHAKY, TOOTHLESS JOE & SICKY.

> WE WISH WE COULD HAVE HELPED YOU
> BUT THIS RIVER'S SO ROUGH
> THE WATERS ARE A-CHURNING SO
> WE KNEW THE BOAT WOULD ROCK
> BUT NEVER DID WE THINK WE'D WIND UP DEAD

> WIND UP DEAD… WIND UP DEAD… WIND UP DEAD!

PHIL THE RAT.

> UP THE RIVER WE WILL SAIL

LIMPY, SHAKY, TOOTHLESS JOE & SICKY.

> *(Overlapping.)* SO LONG, PHIL AND

PHIL THE RAT.

UP THE MOUNTAIN WE WILL CLIMB

LIMPY, SHAKY, TOOTHLESS JOE & SICKY.

(Overlapping.) GOODBYE, DR. WATSON.

PHIL THE RAT.

FROM THE GOLDEN LIGHT OF MORNING

LIMPY, SHAKY, TOOTHLESS JOE & SICKY.

(Overlapping.) HOPE YOU FIND THAT

PHIL THE RAT.

'TIL THE DARK OF EVENING TIME

LIMPY, SHAKY, TOOTHLESS JOE & SICKY.

(Overlapping.) BABY BOY YOU'RE LOOKING FOR AND

PHIL THE RAT.

UP THE OCEAN WE WILL SAIL

LIMPY, SHAKY, TOOTHLESS JOE & SICKY.

(Overlapping.) EAT YOUR VITAMINS AND

PHIL THE RAT.

UP THE ROADWAY WE WILL DRIVE

LIMPY, SHAKY, TOOTHLESS JOE & SICKY.

(Overlapping.) DON'T ROW SO DAMN SLOW

PHIL THE RAT, LIMPY, SHAKY, TOOTHLESS JOE & SICKY.

'CAUSE THAT MEAN OLD RIVER
THAT MEAN OLD RIVER
THAT MEAN OLD RIVER
IS WASHED WITH TALES OF WOE

> *[PROJECTED IMAGES: Images of time passage: the Great Depression, WWII]*

AND THE CLOCK KEEPS ON A PASSING
PASSING THROUGH FROM YEAR TO YEAR
THROUGH ANOTHER CONFLAGRATION
THROUGH ANOTHER CAUSE FOR FEAR

> *[PROJECTED IMAGES: Images of the early 1950s bomb scare]*

THEN WE FOUND OUR DESTINATION
A PLACE OF STONE, A PLACE TO HIDE
IT WAS A PLACE OF DARK PROTECTION

AND THE CHILD WAS THERE INSIDE

[END MUSIC NO. 16]

[PROJECTED TEXT: 1957]

(**PHIL THE RAT** *and* **WATSON** *arrive in a suburban setting.*)

PHIL THE RAT. Right this way, Doctor. He's over here.

(*Scenery and lights clear to reveal the hatch of a bomb shelter.*)

WATSON. Here? In a fallout shelter?

PHIL THE RAT. Haven't you been reading the news? The Russians have the bomb, Doc.

WATSON. They do? I guess I missed that. Traveling around with all the…singers.

(**PHIL THE RAT** *turns the handle of the hatch.*)

PHIL THE RAT. It's open!

(**PHIL THE RAT** *and* **WATSON** *step into the hatch. The stage opens up to reveal the interior of the bomb shelter.*)

[PROJECTED IMAGES: Suggest that the interior of Albert's shelter is wallpapered with newspaper clippings, interviews, and journal articles by and about Watson]

Holy moly. Seems like he's been keeping tabs on you, Doc.

WATSON. Huh. Well, what do you know.

PHIL THE RAT. Every article about you. Everything you've ever written. Looks like you've got yourself a fan.

WATSON. Or maybe not.

(**WATSON** *picks up a book.*)

Introduction to Psychoanalysis by Sigmund Freud.

PHIL THE RAT. It's a trap! Let's get outta here!

(*Suddenly, the hatch slams shut and the stage goes completely black.*)

[MUSIC NO. 16.5 "BOMB SHELTER BLACKOUT"]

WATSON. Phil? Phil? Phil I can't see you. Phil, where are you? PHIL!

> *(In the darkness, we hear* **ALBERT**. *He approaches this encounter as an impartial Freudian analyst would. He is here to help! It is a position he will steadfastly maintain throughout.)*

ALBERT. Don't worry. Your giant talking rat is fine.

WATSON. Albert? Why don't you turn on the lights?

ALBERT. Why?

WATSON. So I can see you.

> (**ALBERT** *steps into a small, dim pool of light.)*

ALBERT. Now you can see me. So what can I do for you, Dr. Watson?

WATSON. I'm…I'm here to help you, Albert. I'm going to remove your fear. After all these years. Then you and I will walk away from this place.

WATSON. Fear?

WATSON. Of…you know… Phil.

ALBERT. Right.

WATSON. And Santa…you know… So…

ALBERT. Dr. Watson, can I ask, why are you afraid of the dark?

> *(Beat.)*

WATSON. Because my mother conditioned me to be, that's why. She used to sing me lullabies about boiling in hell.

ALBERT. That sounds scary.

WATSON. Yes it was. It's very simple, actually, and not dissimilar from –

ALBERT. Dr. Watson. What is in the dark?

> *(Pause.)*

WATSON. Nothing.

ALBERT. But something must be there. Right? *(Beat.)* Do you want me to help you look?

WATSON. How?

ALBERT. Let me analyze you.

WATSON. This is absolutely preposterous, Albert. *I'm* here to help *you.*

ALBERT. But you're not here and neither am I. Or maybe you are. Maybe you did just spend twenty years circling the globe with giant singing rats and have now landed yourself in a bomb shelter and are talking to a fully realized outcome of an incomplete experiment you conducted forty years ago. Or maybe I died when I was five of encephalitis. You see Doctor, this is what I love about the dark. It makes life so much more malleable.

WATSON. Albert, I will not allow this to continue!

> *(Pause.)*

ALBERT. Very well.

> (**ALBERT** *steps out of his light.* **WATSON** *is alone in the dark.)*

WATSON. Albert, don't…! Albert, if I let you do this, will you please turn on the lights.

ALBERT. I will.

WATSON. Very well. Proceed.

> ### [MUSIC NO. 17 "I SURRENDER ALL"]

ALBERT. Just relax, Dr. Watson. Surrender. Look into the emptiness around you. You're right that there's nothing there. Just consciousness. Can't be measured. Can't be quantified. But the more time you spend here maybe you'll find there are things that do start to appear. Memories? Perspective? Regrets?

> (**LIMPY** *and* **SHAKY** *and several other* **RATS** *enter and prepare to sing.)*

RATS.

ALL TO WATSON I SURRENDER
ALL TO THEE I FREELY GIVE

BLIND ME, STARVE ME, SEW MY ASS SHUT
I DON'T MIND IT, NEVER DID.

I SURRENDER ALL

LIMPY.

I MISS MY FEET.

RATS.

I SURRENDER ALL!

LIMPY & SHAKY.

I MISS MY ANUS.

RATS.

ALL TO THEE, MY KING AND MASTER
I SURRENDER ALL.

> *(The music vamps. As* **WATSON** *says the following,
> they begin to remove the outer layer of their
> costume.)*

WATSON. Are you suggesting that I'm haunted by the suffering of the animals who aided in my research?

ALBERT. *I'm* not suggesting anything.

WATSON. That research has led to untold advances in psychology. It has made better the lives of millions of human beings. In fact –

> *(***WATSON** *is interrupted by a chorus of 1950s*
> **CONSUMERS.** *)*

CONSUMERS.

ALL TO WATSON I SURRENDER
ALL MY WISHES NOW ARE HIS
I AM THIRSTY FOR A PEPSI
I AM HUNGRY FOR CHEEZ WHIZ.

I SURRENDER ALL!

SOLOIST.

YOUR PH.D.

CONSUMERS.

I SURRENDER ALL!

SOLOIST.

NOW SELLS THE SLINKY

CONSUMERS.
>ALL TO THEE OPINION MAKER
>I SURRENDER ALL!

WATSON. So you're accusing me of being a sell-out?

ALBERT. Again, Dr. Watson, *I'm* not the one who is suggesting anything.

WATSON. Yes, my impact will be far-reaching. For this I should fear? Your words do nothing but bolster my pride.

>(*The* **CONSUMERS** *disappear into the darkness.*)

ALBERT. Then perhaps we should explore deeper.

WATSON. If you insist.

ALBERT. Deeper, to a darkness that still can't be measured, still can't be quantified. But does that mean it isn't real?

WATSON. Yes, that's what it means.

>(**ROSALIE** *starts to appear in the darkness.* **WATSON** *gradually is able to see her through the following.*)

ALBERT. Is loneliness real?

WATSON. I don't know.

ALBERT. Is loss real?

WATSON. I don't know.

ALBERT. Is love real?

>(**ROSALIE** *is now visible.* **WATSON** *has difficulty containing his emotion.*)

ROSALIE. (*Tenderly.*)
>I SURRENDER ALL
>I SURRENDER ALL
>ALL TO THEE, MY DEAR DEAR JOHN
>I SURRENDER ALL

>(**WATSON** *falls to his knees.* **ROSALIE** *kneels with him.*)

ROSALIE. Don't cry for me, John. I'm not alone or sad or in pain or discomfort. I'm just dead.

There's really nothing that can be done about it. Once you're dead you're all dead.

> (**ROSALIE** *kisses his forehead and fades away, along with the rest of the apparitions. Music continues under the following.* **WATSON** *remains on his knees.*)

WATSON. This is embarrassing.

ALBERT. Why?

WATSON. She died so long ago.

ALBERT. *(Sympathetic.)* This is what you've become, Dr. Watson. An eighty-year-old man who sees his dead wife for the first time in twenty years and feels... embarrassed. If your own thoughts and feelings weren't so alien to you, maybe you would be able to control your behavior.

WATSON. *(Distant.)* Behavior.

> *(The music begins to fade away.)*

ALBERT. Maybe you would have sought me out when I was still here to be found. Maybe you would have offered me...I don't know...an apology. And your kids –

WATSON. *(Snaps and rises to his feet.)* What about them?!

ALBERT. I don't know, Dr. Watson. Maybe they might have had a hug at some point in their childhood?

[END MUSIC NO. 17]

> (**WATSON** *collects himself.*)

WATSON. My kids are well-adjusted and productive members of society, Albert. So, I'm sorry to say I think you're off the mark.

ALBERT. Are they? My mistake then.

WATSON. I lived up to my side of the bargain. I did what I said I was going to do! NOW WILL YOU PLEASE TURN ON THE GODDAMN LIGHTS?!

ALBERT. I will.

(**ALBERT** *flips a switch and the lights snap on to reveal the hallway of a hotel.* **WATSON** *and* **ALBERT**, *in a pool of light, observe* **WILLIAM** *standing outside the door of a room. He knocks. Nothing. He knocks again.*)

WILLIAM. James? James? James, Dad sent me up here to find out what's keeping you. Come on, Jimmy, he's pacing around the lobby. You know how he is about punctuality.

Look, James, I don't want to do this either. But it's his one big night. It's not like he's gonna get the Lifetime Achievement twice. So, look, let's just get this over with and get the hell out of here. Come on, buddy, open the door.

James? *(A tone shift.)* James, I'm begging you, please open the door. Don't make me do it alone.

(*The door opens to reveal* **JAMES**, *disheveled and bleeding from one of his wrists.*)

Holy shit. What are you doing? James, what are you doing?

JAMES. I'm sorry, Bill.

WILLIAM. James…

JAMES. I can't take it any more. It's time I put a stop to it… for everyone.

WILLIAM. James, wait a minute. James, what are you doing?

JAMES. What do you think I'm doing? I'm killing myself, Bill.

WILLIAM. Killing yourself??

JAMES. Yes!

WILLIAM. You can't.

JAMES. I most certainly can.

WILLIAM. You can't kill yourself, Jimmy.

JAMES. It's not your decision!

WILLIAM. You can't kill yourself.

JAMES. Why not?

WILLIAM. Because I'm already killing *my*-self.

    (A tiny beat.)

JAMES. What?!

WILLIAM. I'm in the middle of killing myself right now.

JAMES. Wait, what?

WILLIAM. I'm killing myself.

JAMES. You're killing *your*-self?

WILLIAM. Yes.

JAMES. Again?

WILLIAM. Yes!

JAMES. I can't believe this.

WILLIAM. It's true. I started about a half an hour ago. And God knows we can't BOTH kill ourselves, so clean yourself up and get your ass downstairs.

JAMES. You don't *look* like you're killing yourself.

WILLIAM. What's that supposed to mean?

JAMES. I don't know. Look, I'm just saying that when people are killing themselves they look like it.

WILLIAM. I took poison.

JAMES. Really?

WILLIAM. Yes.

JAMES. Honestly?

WILLIAM. *(Exasperated.)* Yes!

    (A tiny beat.)

JAMES. You're always killing yourself. It's obnoxious, you know.

WILLIAM. You should talk.

JAMES. At least my attempts are serious! Your suicides are just cries for help!

WILLIAM. Are not!

JAMES. Are too!

    (WATSON *steps into the scene, leaving* **ALBERT** *behind in the pool of light.)*

WATSON. Enough! Nobody here is killing themselves and that's final.

WILLIAM. Dad!

JAMES. Hey Dad.

WATSON. *(Calmly.)* James. Find a sterile cloth and apply direct pressure for five or six minutes. Go. I'd be willing to bet there's another towel in the bathroom. I'll fetch some gauze or bandaging from the front desk. I said go.

JAMES. Good to see you, Dad.

> *(A moment of hesitation before **JAMES** exits to the bathroom. A pause.)*

WILLIAM. How's it going?

WATSON. What did you take?

WILLIAM. Phenobarbital.

WATSON. How much?

WILLIAM. Three grams.

WATSON. I see.

> *(**WATSON** heads for the lobby.)*

WILLIAM. Where are you going?

WATSON. I'm afraid your brother was right. As I'm sure you know, a lethal dose of Phenobarbital would require nearly double that amount.

WILLIAM. Three grams was all I had.

WATSON. Yes, well…no matter.

WILLIAM. Dad? *(Pause.)* Where have you been all these years?

> *(**WATSON** glances briefly at **ALBERT**.)*

WATSON. Working.

WILLIAM. On what?

WATSON. An experiment.

WILLIAM. How did it go?

WATSON. I don't know.

WILLIAM. Did you finish it?

WATSON. I don't know.

WILLIAM. Well...what were you trying to do?

> *(The light winks out on* **ALBERT***.)*

WATSON. *(With resignation.)* I don't know.

> *(Beat.)*

WILLIAM. Missed you, Dad.

> *(Short pause.)*

WATSON. I need to get that gauze.

> *(***WATSON*** moves to exit again.)*

WILLIAM. Does it matter to you at all that we're miserable?

> *(***WATSON*** stops.)*

WATSON. It matters.

> *(***WATSON***, moved, heads toward* **WILLIAM***.)*

I'm sorry I missed it, Bill.

> *(On the verge of an embrace,* **WATSON** *abandons it. He is incapable after all these years.)*

I mean, tell them...I mean, let them know...tell them... let them know I'm sorry but I'm going to have to miss the ceremony.

> *(***WATSON*** exits. As the* **CHORUS** *enters to carry out the transition, they are shaken and bewildered. Some seem to forget why they are there.)*

[MUSIC NO. 18 "SCIENCE IS HARD"]

TENOR SOLOIST.	CHORUS.
SCIENCE IS HARD	OOOH
YOU MAY SPEND YOUR WHOLE LIFE SEEKING TRUTH	OOH
'TIL YOU LEARN THAT ALL YOU KNOW	OOH
IS A LIE	IS A LIE

CHORUS.

> GO AND FIND A PLACE TO HIDE
> AND CONTEMPLATE YOUR SAD AFFAIRS
> A FARM OUT IN CONNECTICUT
> WHERE YOU'LL DRINK AWAY YOUR CARES
>
> YOUR AMBITION IS SCARRED
> ALL YOUR DATA IS CHARRED
> YOU WERE CAUGHT OFF YOUR GUARD
> SCIENCE IS HARD

> *[END MUSIC NO. 18]*

> *[PROJECTED TEXT: Watson's farm in Westport, Connecticut – 1958]*

> *(A barn. The* **CHORUS** *has transformed into* **DOGS**, **HORSES**, *and other barnyard* **ANIMALS** *who are getting drunk.* **WATSON** *is throwing papers onto a fire while they're singing.* **DOG** *is helping him.)*

> *[MUSIC NO. 19 "DRINKING SONG"]*

HORSE.

> LIFE IS A WASTE OF TIME,
> TIME IS A WASTE OF LIFE,
> SO GET WASTED ALL OF THE TIME
> AND HAVE THE TIME OF YOUR LIFE. EVERYBODY!

> *(PHIL THE RAT enters and observes the scene with sadness.)*

ALL ANIMALS.

> LIFE IS A WASTE OF TIME,
> TIME IS A WASTE OF LIFE,
> SO GET WASTED ALL OF THE TIME
> AND HAVE THE TIME OF YOUR LIFE

> *(They all empty their glasses and hoot, howl, and squeak.)*

PHIL THE RAT. Dr. Watson, maybe we should head inside now.

WATSON. Bullshit, Phil. We're just getting started here, right boy?

DOG. Aaaoooo!!

ALL ANIMALS. Aaaoooo!!

> (**PHIL THE RAT** *picks one of the papers off the ground.*)

PHIL THE RAT. No. No!! What are you doing, Doc? These are your papers! Your data, Doc! You're burning all of your data.

WATSON. They were cold.

RABBIT. Yeah, we were cold.

PHIL THE RAT. People are going to need this, Doc. How are they going to piece it all together?

WATSON. Piece what together?

PHIL THE RAT. The ideas! The science! Your dream.

WATSON. Oh, dear Phil. That dream is over.

PHIL THE RAT. I don't understand.

WATSON. Well, let me put it this way…

> (*Lighting becomes even more theatrical. A follow spot opens on* **WATSON**. *He begins to sing a drinking song of his own.*)

[MUSIC NO. 20 "ONCE YOU'RE DEAD, YOU'RE ALL DEAD"]

ONCE YOU'RE DEAD, YOU'RE ALL DEAD
DON'T WORRY YOUR FURRY SMALL HEAD
YOUR DREAMS HAVE BEEN DREAMED
YOUR WORDS HAVE BEEN READ
AND ONCE YOU'RE DEAD, YOU'RE ALL DEAD

WATSON.	**ANIMALS.**
ONCE YOU FOUND SOME ACCLAIM	OOOOH
FROM THOUSANDS WHO HONORED	
YOUR NAME	
IT WAS ONLY A GAME	
SO LET'S GET DRUNK INSTEAD	
'CAUSE ONCE YOU'RE DEAD,	
YOU'RE ALL DEAD	

ALL ANIMALS. Aaaaoooo!!

(The **ANIMALS** *[except* **PHIL THE RAT***] throw more papers in the fire as they sing.)*

ALL ANIMALS.

ONCE HE'S DEAD, HE'S ALL DEAD
DON'T WORRY OUR FURRY SMALL HEADS
HIS DREAMS HAVE BEEN DREAMED
HIS WORDS HAVE BEEN READ
AND ONCE HE'S DEAD, HE'S ALL DEAD

(The **ANIMALS** *leap to their feet and dance around the fire. They throw more papers as the flames grow bigger and brighter.* **WATSON** *joins them until he suddenly becomes tired and sits. The* **ANIMALS** *gather around him, as* **WATSON** *sings to* **PHIL THE RAT***.)*

WATSON.

SO WARM YOUR HANDS BY THE FIRE
REFLECT ON WHAT DID TRANSPIRE
REFLECT ON THE EMBERS THAT GLOW IN THE NIGHT
THAT DANCE ON THE BREEZE
'TIL THEY FADE OUT OF SIGHT
REFLECT ON A WORLD THAT DEFIED YOUR CONTROL
THAT BROKE FROM YOUR GRASP,
AND THEN SWALLOWED YOU WHOLE
SURRENDER LIKE EMBERS INSTEAD
FOR ONCE YOU'RE DEAD, YOU'RE ALL DEAD
ONCE YOU'RE DEAD…

*(***WATSON** *quietly lowers his head and dies. Pause. Music shifts.)*

[MUSIC NO. 21 "FINALE"]

PHIL THE RAT.

WE KNOW THAT WE KNOW NOTHING
WE KNOW WE KNOW IT ALL
OUR HOPES, THEY WILL SUSTAIN US
OR THEY WILL MAKE US FALL

(**WATSON** *"wakes" and watches the others.*
ROSALIE *appears, presented as if she is an exhibit.*)

ROSALIE.

I KNOW THAT WATER BOILS
AND I KNOW IT WILL FREEZE
I KNOW SUNSETS ARE USELESS
I KNOW THAT THEY PLEASE

(**ALBERT** *appears, a second exhibit.*)

ALBERT.

I KNOW I WAS CONDITIONED
TO FEEL WHAT I FEEL
I KNOW THAT IT WAS FAKE
AND I KNOW IT WAS REAL

CHORUS.

THE LESSONS FELL SHORT.
ONLY QUESTIONS REMAIN
AND SO WE WILL DRIFT LIKE AN EMBER UP INTO THE SKY
THE CLOUDS
THE MOUNTAINS, THE CANYONS
THE BOTTOMLESS OCEAN
ACROSS THE WIDE PLAIN

PAST THE MOON
THE STARS
THE VASTNESS OF SPACE
THE INFINITE DARKNESS
THE TINIEST CELL OF OUR BRAIN

(*During the preceding, through* **Projections**, *the
stage has been filled with* **images of grandeur from
the earth and the universe**. *The* **CHORUS** *and*
WATSON *seem very small indeed as they stare in
wonder at the universe around them. A bright light
appears before* **WATSON**. *He slowly walks into it.*)

THREE STEPS TO THE LEFT
FIVE STEPS STRAIGHT AHEAD

THREE STEPS TO THE LEFT
FIVE STEPS STRAIGHT AHEAD
THREE STEPS TO THE LEFT
FIVE STEPS STRAIGHT AHEAD

[END MUSIC NO. 21]

(**WATSON** *exits the space. Blackout.*)

[MUSIC NO. 22 "PAPER AND PEN (BOWS)"]

End of Play